SERIES

Chief Honor

SIGMUND BROUWER

WORD PUBLISHING
Dallas•London•Vancouver•Melbourne

To Durkee—
Finally one for you.

CHIEF HONOR
Copyright © 1997 by Sigmund Brouwer.

Published in Nashville, Tennessee, by Tommy Nelson®,
a division of Thomas Nelson, Inc.
Visit us on the Web at www.tommynelson.com

Library of Congress Cataloging-in-Publication Data

Brouwer, Sigmund, 1959–
    Chief honor / Sigmund Brouwer.
        p.   cm.—(Lightning on ice series ; 6)
    Summary: Joseph "Gump" Larken, goalie for the Spokane Chiefs,
is not bothered by playing second string to the first woman in the
Western Hockey League, but he is not certain how to handle the
accusation that his closest friend on the team might be involved
with illegal steroids.
    ISBN 0-8499-3984-4
    [1. Hockey—Fiction. 2. Steroids—Fiction.] I. Title. II. Series:
Brouwer, Sigmund, 1959–   Lightning on ice series ; 6.
PZ7.B79984Ch   1997
[Fic]—dc21

                                                                96–48592
                                                                    CIP
                                                                     AC

Printed in the United States of America
00 01 02 03 04 PHX 13 12 11 10 09

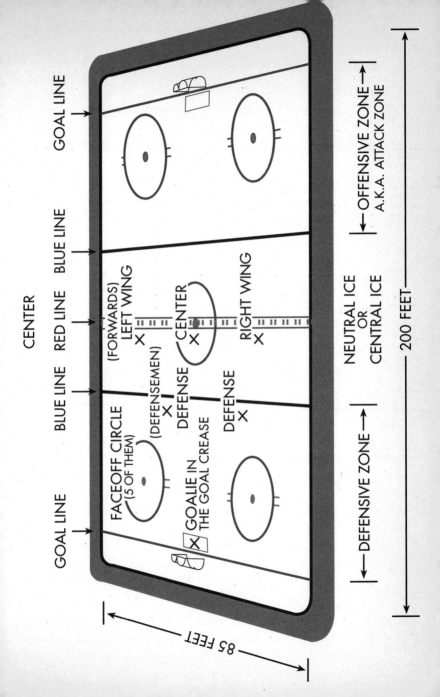

Hockey Terms

For readers new to hockey, the following definitions may be helpful.

Assist: A player earns an assist by making a pass that is converted into a goal.

Blue line, red line, goal line: The length of the ice is roughly divided into thirds. One third up the ice from each end a blue line crosses the ice. The red line crosses the ice at the halfway point. At each of the far ends, a goal line crosses the ice (see diagram on page v).

Boards: The entire ice surface is enclosed by waist-high boards that are curved in the corners to match the oval of the rink. A Plexiglas shield above the boards protects the spectators from being hit by a stray puck.

Body check: In hockey, it is legal to run into the person with the puck as long as contact is made with the upper body or hips.

Breakaway: A breakaway occurs when a player with the puck has no one between him and the opposing goalie.

Faceoff: A faceoff occurs at the beginning of each period and after each stoppage of play. The referee drops the puck to start play, and the center from each team tries to gain control of the puck.

Forechecker: When a forward or forwards are sent deep into the offensive zone after the puck or puck carrier, they are called forecheckers.

Hipcheck: A hipcheck is similar to a body check except contact is made as the hip is swung outward.

Icing: An icing penalty is called when a player shoots from behind his blue line and the puck travels all the way across the goal line at the far end. It results in a faceoff in the player's own end, which cancels the advantage of having moved the puck so far.

One-time: The process of hitting the puck without first stopping it.

Overtime: Overtime rules vary in different leagues. In the WHL, it consists of ten minutes of extra play. The first team to score in the extra time wins the game (called sudden-death overtime). In regular season play, a tie at the end of overtime remains a tie. In playoff games, overtime is played until a goal is scored to break the tie.

Period: A regular hockey game consists of sixty minutes of play, divided into three twenty-minute periods.

Point: (1) A single point is given for a goal. (2) In team standings, zero points are accumulated for a loss, one point for a tie, and two points for a win. (3) When a defenseman is standing inside the opposition's blue line, his position is also referred to as "standing at the point."

Power play: Penalties in hockey result in the offending player "serving time" in the penalty box. This time varies according to the penalty. With one and sometimes two fewer players on the ice, the penalized team is at a tremendous disadvantage. The unpenalized team is then considered on the power play. It is also known as a "man advantage" or a "two-man advantage."

Slap shot: A slap shot is the hardest shot in hockey. A player raises his stick above his shoulders before swinging downward to "slap" the shot. Slap shots have been recorded at speeds of well over 100 miles per hour.

Stickhandle: To control the puck by moving it from side to side with the blade of the hockey stick.

Two-on-one, three-on-one, four-on-one, and so on: If there is only one defenseman between the goalie and two attackers with the puck, it is called a "two-on-one"; the other numbers correspond to the various situations.

Zone: The ice surface is broken into three zones. The areas behind each of the two blue lines are known as the end zones; the central area between both blue lines is the neutral zone.

One

"Hey, Gump!" The yell came from one of my Spokane Chiefs teammates, standing beside me in the players' box. "Gump! I gotta tell you about the hot chocolate!"

I ignored him. One of the reasons was the hockey game in front of me. The hockey game I wanted to be playing in.

"Gump! Gump!"

Another reason I ignored him is partly why I have my nickname: Gump the Grump.

I'm not only grumpy, I'm also short and wide. Actually, if people want to be mean, they can call me fat and be close to right. Short, wide guys normally don't have much of a chance in sports. But I have two things going for me. I don't feel pain. And I have quick hands.

Both of these things help in my sport. A lot. I face other guys who are taller and faster. At times, they skate almost 30 miles an hour. They fire a hard rubber disk at speeds of over 100 miles per hour—at me, Joseph Larken. I'm a goalie in the Western Hockey League, which is one step short of the National Hockey League. Newspapers say I am one of the best in the league. But I wasn't going to play tonight. All because of a new goalie. A girl. Lauren Cross.

Tonight I was a backup goalie. My job at the moment was to open and close the door for skaters as they stepped on and off the ice. We were playing our final exhibition game of the preseason against the Portland Winter Hawks. There were still a few cuts to be made, so the players who weren't sure if they had made the team would be busting extra hard tonight.

"Hey, Gump!"

I finally pulled my eyes away from the action against the Portland Winter Hawks. A couple of our guys were forechecking* hard in the other team's end.

"What is it?" I asked Eddie Dyer. The guy had his head bent down to my ear and had been yelling above the noise of the crowd to get my attention. Last year, Eddie hadn't been strong enough to make the team. This year he was stronger and bigger, a lot bigger, like he could be a model for a body building magazine. It was almost certain he would make the team this year.

"Betcha ten bucks you're in the game by the end of the period*," he said.

"Nope," I told him, staring into a face dotted with big, purple pimples.

---

* An asterisk in the text indicates a hockey term that is in the list of definitions on pages vi–viii.

"Yup," he said. Sweat made his pimples seem even bigger. "All the guys want you in the net. By the end of the period, she'll be gone. You'll be playing. Not her. Just wait and see."

"I meant 'nope' I won't bet." A backup goaltender only plays if the other goalie gets hurt or plays bad. Much as I wanted to play, I wasn't going to hope either one happened to her.

Eddie grinned at me. "You're a smart man."

"Smart?"

"Smart not to bet. Did you figure out the hot chocolate already?"

"What?" I had to shout. The crowd was cheering on its home team. In the Winter Hawks' arena, the noise is louder than a landing jet.

"The hot chocolate. One of the guys thought of it yesterday and—" Eddie stopped yelling and stepped away from me. Two of our skaters were heading toward the players' box. They needed a rest.

I yanked the door open. They stepped into the box as two other players jumped over the boards* and raced toward the action. On the other side of the ice, a Winter Hawks defenseman had just passed the puck ahead to his center. The Winter Hawks were at full speed and headed to our end of the ice.

I felt Eddie lean toward me again. He shouted, "The hot chocolate you gave her. It's—"

"Hang on a second!" I shouted back without looking at him. My eyes were on the game as the Winter Hawks moved the puck into our zone*. I wanted to learn as much as I could about their offense. I wanted to know how they moved the puck around. Playing or not playing, I always look for things that give away shooters' secrets.

The Winter Hawks center uncorked a slap shot* from just inside the blue line*. He was probably thinking what everyone else was thinking. *A girl in net. Shoot from anywhere.*

But he didn't know what I knew. While the papers were making a big deal about a girl in net, they were forgetting the real story. Lauren Cross was good. Real good.

The slap shot was a low hard screamer. It hit the stick of one of our defensemen, and the puck deflected up. It was a blur headed toward the high right corner of our net.

It was going in . . . was going in . . . it was . . .

Like a cobra, Lauren's glove flashed upward and snagged the puck. She pulled the puck in close to her body.

The ref blew the whistle to stop the play.

Even though this was a Portland crowd, everyone went wild. Not only was it Lauren's first save of the game, but it was also her first save in the WHL, even if it was only preseason. A lot of the crowd was here because of all the publicity about a girl in the net. It was the kind of publicity that was selling tickets. But if it sold too many tickets, I stood a good chance of spending less time in the net myself.

"Don't worry, Gump," Eddie yelled into my ear. "Even

with saves like that, she'll be gone by the end of the period."

The referee skated to the net and took the puck from Lauren to get ready for a faceoff*. Both teams made line changes. It gave me time to look back at Eddie.

"Okay," I said to Eddie. "What do you mean? And what about the hot chocolate?"

He grinned at me. "Remember the hot chocolate before the game?"

I remembered. The bus had gotten here early. With some time to kill, we had all hung around the front lobby of the arena. The concessions stand wasn't open yet. Some of the guys were drinking pop they bought from a machine. Others were drinking hot chocolate from another vending machine. Eddie had brought me two cups and told me to give one to Lauren. She'd looked lonely standing by herself at the other side of the lobby. She smiled when I gave it to her. I think she was worried that I hated her for getting all the attention.

"And remember how I told you to make sure she got the one with extra sugar?" Eddie asked.

I told him I remembered that too. The one in my right hand. Eddie had made a big deal that I give her the cup from my right hand.

Eddie looked over to make sure Coach Mead wasn't listening.

"Well," Eddie said, putting his mouth close to my ear. "That cup had extra sugar, all right. To hide the taste of the Ex-Lax in it. Lots of super-strength chocolate-flavored Ex-Lax."

"Huh?" I said.

"Ex-Lax. You know, a laxative. The stuff that old people use when they need to clear their insides."

"Why?" I said.

"It puts them on the toilet," he said. "In a hurry."

I shook my head at his stupidity. "I meant why did you do that to her?"

"Don't you get it? We wanted you to start tonight. We figured it would hit her before the game and she wouldn't be able to start. But this is even better."

"Even better?" I could hardly believe him.

"Come on," he said. "You of all people know how tough it is to be trapped in goalie equipment."

He grinned an ugly grin. "Think of what that Ex-Lax is doing to her. Any time now, she's going to have to get out of all that gear in a big, big hurry!"

Two

A big, big hurry? There's hardly anything a goalie can do in a big, big hurry.

Think about carrying around two big bags of flour. Then imagine wrapping yourself in layer after layer of tape so that you can barely walk. That's what it's like to wear goalie equipment.

Everything a goalie wears is heavier than regular equipment. The skates have bigger blades and steel toes. You wear wide leg pads. Heavy hockey pants. A chest protector. An extra-large sweater. A throat protector. A face mask. A goalie helmet. A blocking pad to guard your arm over your stick hand. A padded catching glove on the other hand. In all that gear, you can stand there, fall down, do the splits, shoot out your hands, or dive one way or the other. But hurry to the bathroom? No way.

I watched Lauren. I thought of the half hour it takes to get dressed for a game. I thought of how long it takes to remove all that equipment. And I hoped nothing would happen to her until the buzzer at the end of the first period.

"Hey, Gump." Eddie nudged me. "Look! She's starting to dance!"

He didn't have to tell me. I knew already. Lauren, in all that heavy gear, had started to hop and push back and forth from one skate to the other.

Eddie laughed. I didn't. I had the sick feeling you get when you see a car accident about to happen and can't do anything to stop it.

You see, goalies are different from other hockey players. We never cheer against each other. Why? Only goalies truly know what it's like to be a goalie. Because you're the last player between the puck and the net, the blame always falls on you when the other team scores a goal. I mean, just watch the sports highlights on television. Do you ever see the great saves? Hardly ever. More like goal after goal after goal after goal.

Bad as it is when someone scores a good goal against you, it's worse if you let in a soft goal. It's such an awful feeling, you never want it to happen to anyone else. Although I wanted my job back, I wanted it because I play well. Not because of something Lauren might do wrong.

Lauren hopped and danced more. The puck was in the Winter Hawks' end, and she was starting to go crazy between the goal posts at our end.

Eddie giggled and punched my arm. "Any time now!" he said.

I wanted to bury my head. But, just like watching a car accident, I could not turn my head away.

Lauren slapped her leg pads with her stick. I imagined the pain she felt. I guessed she slapped her pads because she was trying to take her mind off what her body wanted to do.

She slapped her leg pads again. Harder. There were five minutes left in the first period. Could she last that long?

I looked back at the players fighting for the puck in the Winter Hawks' end. Maybe the play would stop soon and the ref would blow the whistle. Then, at least, she could skate off the ice between plays.

But it looked bad. The Winter Hawks defensemen were passing the puck around. No chance for a whistle.

I looked back at Lauren.

She had stopped dancing and was bent over in pain. *How much longer could she wait?*

I turned to watch the puck. One of the Winter Hawks defensemen passed the puck up the boards to a winger.

I snapped my head back to Lauren. Except she wasn't in the net. She was racing full speed toward our players' box.

The crowd noticed too. People began screaming. This had never happened before. *A goalie leaving in the middle of a play?*

Halfway to the blue line, Lauren dropped her stick. Still skating hard, she threw her blocker off one hand and her catching glove off the other. One more step and she flung her face mask off her head. She left it all behind her like litter falling from a moving car.

One of our defensemen, skating backward, tripped over her stick. The other defenseman tripped over the first as he sprawled on the ice.

Lauren didn't care. Didn't even know. Her arms were pumping as she skated with desperation.

At our blue line, she nearly hit the Winter Hawks forward who was racing toward our net with the puck. I caught the look of surprise on his face. *A goalie leaving the net faster than he was skating toward it?*

It didn't matter to Lauren.

"Open up," she screamed from thirty feet away. "Open up!"

Behind her, surprised or not, the Winter Hawks forward skated past the two fallen defensemen and dumped the puck into the open net.

"Open up!" she yelled from twenty feet away. I don't think she cared that they had just scored against her. Not with what she needed to do.

Our coach was yelling. Our assistant coach was yelling. The fans were yelling. No one knew what was happening except for the players in on the joke. And, of course, Lauren.

"Open up!" she screamed again from ten feet away. Her long red hair was flowing straight behind her. Her face was tight with pain. "Open up!"

I yanked the gate open just before Lauren got to the bench.

She jumped into the players' box. She dove past

me. Past Eddie. Past the coaches. She hit the hallway running.

"Well," Eddie said above all of the noise and confusion, "that takes care of that problem, doesn't it?"

Something about his mean grin got to me. "You're an idiot," I said. "An ugly, stupid idiot."

His face twisted and turned purple. He jumped on top of me and wrapped his fingers around my neck. He began to choke me.

Three

At the end of the game, reporters stuck microphones in my face the second I sat down in the dressing room. Their questions hit me like hailstones.

"What's it like to play second-string goalie behind a girl?"

"Can you tell us why she left the game?"

"Were you happy to see Lauren Cross leave in such a hurry?"

"Is it true that the coach started her tonight because you're overweight?"

"Do you think your father was listening to the game on the radio?"

"Are you and Lauren friends off the ice?"

"Give us your opinion on her goaltending skills."

Sharks. All of them. There was Steve Haliburton, the newspaper reporter who followed us on the road. Two reporters from radio stations. And, worst of all, a woman reporter from a television station. That's one thing I didn't get. Why were women allowed in the dressing room? It was like that in sports everywhere. Women would sue if they weren't allowed in the dressing rooms with the men reporters.

Steve, the guy from the newspaper, stuck a tape recorder almost into my mouth. "It looked like one of your teammates jumped you when Lauren left the ice," he said. "I think it was Eddie Dyer. Can you tell us about that?"

Sudden silence. He must have been the only one who noticed. The others, I guessed, wanted to hear my answer so they could add it to their stories.

"We played a hard game," I told him. He was tall and skinny with a beak nose. He was nearly bald. He grew his remaining hair long and slicked it sideways over his head.

"Although we lost," I continued, "we gave it our best shot. And win or lose, this is a team game. A couple of bounces our way instead of theirs, and it might have been a different game tonight."

As I spoke, I kept the anger out of my voice. What gave them the right to ask such rude questions? *Is it true that the coach started her because you're overweight? Do you think your father was listening to the game on the radio? Are you and Lauren friends off the ice?*

"Huh?" the television reporter said. She looked at her notebook. "Joseph Larken, right? What kind of answer is that?"

"She's new," I heard one reporter say. "She doesn't know about Gump the Grump."

Steve said, "Come on, Gump. Give us a break. Was there a fight on the bench?"

No law said I had to answer any of their questions. So I repeated myself. "We played a hard game. Although we lost, we gave it our best shot. And win or lose, this is a team game. A couple of bounces our way instead of theirs, and it might have been a different game tonight."

"Get real," the television reporter said. "What about you and the girl goaltender? Anything happening there?"

Her cameraman behind her clicked on the bright light to film my answer.

"I'm sorry," I said to her, noticing red in her fake smile, "but didn't your cameraman tell you about the lipstick on your teeth?"

She gave me a dirty look. But she hissed at the cameraman to cut the shot. She backed away and grabbed a small mirror from her purse. The others crowded in.

"Was there a fight on the bench?"

"Why did Lauren Cross leave the game?"

"Who's a better goalie. You or her?"

These guys didn't know I had learned plenty about dealing with news people. This was playing marbles with little kids compared to the heat I had taken back home during the summer. Nothing these sports reporters could do would rattle me. Nothing they asked could get a reaction out of me.

"We played a hard game," I told all of them. "Although we lost, we gave it our best shot. And win or lose, this is a team game. A couple of bounces our way instead of theirs, and it might have been a different game tonight."

That's what I had learned about dealing with news reporters. Give them short answers that they couldn't twist. Repeat those short answers very politely. Smile through the anger. If you did anything else, they would make you look like an idiot in their stories.

"Get serious Larken," one of the radio guys said. "What about the fight in the box. We need answers."

"Answers? It's 93 million miles to the sun," I said, still smiling. "If you traveled at the speed of light, you would get to the sun in less than ten minutes. The moon does not consist of cheese. Water is made of hydrogen and oxygen. Two plus two equals—"

"Huh?" The woman reporter was back. I don't think she understood sarcasm.

"Your nylons," I said. "Big run in them."

She glared at me. Then quickly looked down at her legs.

"Hockey answers," the radio guy said.

I smiled. "We played a hard game. Although we lost, we gave it our best shot. And win or lose, this is a team game. A couple of bounces our way instead of theirs, and it might have been a different game tonight."

They all left. All at once. Like none of them could think without the others. I noticed the newspaper guy heading for Eddie Dyer.

"It looked like you jumped Larken in the box when Lauren Cross left the game," I heard Steve Haliburton say to Eddie. "What happened?"

"I fell," Eddie said, "right on top of him. Lauren tripped me as she ran past, and I fell."

"But it looked like you were swinging at him until a couple of your teammates grabbed you."

"They were trying to help me get off him," Eddie said. "Pretty easy mistake, I guess, thinking it was a fight."

If Eddie wanted to lie, that was his business. The guys had pulled him off me, and Coach had sent me onto the ice to play.

"That's cool," a radio reporter said to Eddie. "Any idea why Lauren left the game?"

"Maybe an upset stomach because of the pressure," Eddie said. "She hasn't said anything, but that's my guess."

What an idiot. I shook my head and began to untie my skates. *What a stupid, ugly idiot.*

I didn't find out until later there was a reason for his stupidity. And when I did find out, it nearly cost me everything.

Four

"Joseph, this is your mother."

Like who else would be on the telephone at *exactly* noon on Sunday?

"Hello," I said. I didn't sit down on the chair beside the telephone. I stayed standing. The television room was small, so there wasn't much room for someone my size to pace.

"So," she said, "how was church today?"

I was glad I was alone upstairs. These weekly phone calls were always painful.

"I didn't go," I said. *Why couldn't she just ask if I went instead of trying to find the answer by coming at it sideways?*

"Oh," she said. She made sure with one short word that I could tell her feelings were hurt.

I could picture what she looked like. I knew the hurt look she wore on her face whenever I disappointed her. She was short, like me, with brown hair, like me, and she frowned a lot, like me.

I waited for Mom to get to the next part.

The door to the television room was open. Downstairs in the kitchen, I could hear old Mr. and Mrs. DuPont as they clattered dishes getting lunch ready. In WHL hockey, out-of-town players live with local people; we call them billets. The DuPonts were great billets. I had the upstairs of the house to myself, and they always offered me plenty to eat. Which I always did.

"You told me this was the last week of exhibition games. How is it going?" Mom asked. Her question didn't fool me. I knew she didn't care about my hockey. She only asked to kill time before getting to the other stuff. "Last night, weren't you playing . . ."

"Portland," I told her. "The Winter Hawks. I played net the last two periods. And we lost."

I didn't tell her that one of our own players had tried to strangle me. And I sure didn't tell her about the Ex-Lax and how Lauren Cross had missed most of the game.

"Didn't I read somewhere about a girl trying out for your team?" she asked.

I was surprised she knew that much. The only thing she keeps track of in hockey is my schedule, like she wants to know what I'm doing every single second of my life.

"Yes, you did," I said. "It looks like she's going to make the team. There's so much in the newspapers about her that—"

"That's nice," my mother said. It sounded as if her mind were some place else. And I could guess where.

"Your father misses you," she said.

I had guessed right. I didn't say anything though. No matter what I told her about my feelings, my mother never listened to me.

"He really misses you," my mother tried again.

I heard the doorbell ring downstairs.

"It looks like our team might have a good year," I said. It always happened this way. Her talking about my father. Me trying to change the subject.

"I wish you wouldn't be like that," she said.

"Like what?" Although I knew what she meant.

"Whenever we talk about your father, you get this tone in your voice. You really should—"

"Hang on," I said. Footsteps were coming up the stairs. It didn't sound like the old and slow footsteps of the DuPonts.

"Hang on? This is your mother you are speaking to."

"I'm sorry," I said. "It's just that someone is here."

"A visitor? For you? At the DuPonts? Who? It's not a girl, is it?"

The visitor made it to the hallway. The visitor made it to the doorway of the television room. I waved at her. Lauren Cross. She wasn't smiling.

"Who is it?" my mother asked again.

"Someone from the team," I said. Lauren definitely wasn't smiling. "I need to go."

"Joseph," my mother said, "please, just think about visiting your father."

19

"I'll think about it," I said.

"I'll talk to you next Sunday, then."

"Sure," I said.

"Good-bye then," she said. "And remember, you promised to think about visiting your father."

"Sure," I said. "Good-bye."

I hung up the phone. I'd think about my father like I promised. And then I'd decide there was no way in the world I would visit him. For all I cared, he could stay in that prison for the rest of his life.

Five

"H ello," I said to Lauren.

She is a little taller than me, but then a lot of people are. Her hair is thick and long and red. She has a lean face. Although she isn't beautiful like a model, she has big, dark eyes that make her face nice to look at.

"Hello?" I said again.

She remained in the doorway and stared at me from those dark eyes.

I stayed by the phone. It's a small room. I was at the back wall, with a big easy chair beside me. Against one side wall is the television and a bookshelf. Against the other side wall is a chair facing the television. Behind it are more shelves, filled with hockey souvenirs, like medals and photos and hockey pucks signed by players from Spokane Chiefs teams of earlier years.

"Um, hello?" I tried again.

A strange look crossed her face. "I thought I would

be able to talk to you without losing my temper," she said. "But I was wrong."

She stepped through the doorway, turned sideways, and grabbed a hockey puck from the shelf. She fired it at my head.

Without thinking—because there was no time to—I snapped my right hand upward and caught the puck. It stopped a half inch from my eye.

She moved toward me. It only took two steps to reach me. Her eyes burned with anger. She slapped her hand toward my face.

I snapped my left hand upward and caught her wrist.

With her other hand, she slapped again. Both my hands were already full. I could not stop her. I took her slap across my face.

I blinked.

"Do something," she hissed. "Yell, fight back."

"I don't hit girls," I said.

She punched me in the stomach. "But you'll put Ex-Lax in their hot chocolate!"

She lifted her leg to stomp on my toes. She was wearing boots. I was wearing socks. I dropped her wrist and the puck and grabbed her shoulders. I twisted her sideways. It wasn't that I was worried about the pain. I just didn't want any of my toes broken. And she seemed mad enough to break them.

"Will you please sit down?" I asked, holding her shoulders as she wriggled. I'm short and wide, but I'm not weak.

"You are scum, Joseph Larken!"

"Will you please sit down?"

Maybe because my voice stayed calm, she did. She took the chair that faced the television. I took the easy chair.

"I know what you did," she said. Although she had stopped trying to hurt me, her voice was still hot with anger.

"What makes you think you know?"

"Eddie Dyer told me," she said. "He told me how you wanted me out of the game, so you put Ex-Lax in my hot chocolate. He told me that's why he jumped you."

"What?"

"He thought you were a jerk for doing it. He said you laughed when I left the ice and he couldn't help getting mad at you for it."

"What!" If Eddie were in front of me, I would have strangled him right then. *Why had he told her it was my idea? Why had he lied?*

"What if I told you I didn't know the Ex-Lax was in there?"

"I wouldn't believe you," she said. "Who else would want me out of the game?"

She shook her head. Anger left her face. Disgust replaced it. "I thought you were so sweet when you gave me that hot chocolate. All the guys were standing around, and I didn't want to force myself on them to make myself part of the group. When you gave me the hot chocolate, it was like an invitation to be a friend. It tasted horrible, but I didn't want to insult you by throwing it away. And then I found out why you really gave it to me . . ."

"I didn't know anything was in there," I said quietly. I wasn't going to blame anyone else, but I had to at least tell her it wasn't me.

"I expected tough times." She went on as if she hadn't heard me. "I knew it wouldn't be easy. I've worked out with weights since I was ten. I had my dad and my brother shoot pucks at me every summer in our backyard. I was ready to prove I could do it."

"I didn't know it was in there," I said again.

"And I can do it." She wasn't listening to me. "Manon Rheaume is playing pro hockey. If she can do it, so can I. So don't think your little trick is going to stop me."

"Listen to me," I said. "Yes, I gave you the hot chocolate, but I didn't know what was in it."

"You expect me to believe you? Like I don't know about your father? I guess cheating and lying runs in the family."

I took a deep breath. A real deep breath. My hands began to shake. I didn't trust myself to speak.

"You are total scum," she said, standing. "I came here to tell you that. I also came here to tell you something else. We are now enemies. Whatever it takes, I'm going to make sure I'm this team's goalie. Not you. I may be a girl, but you're fat and you're scum."

With that, she stomped out of the room.

A few minutes later, I stood too. I went over to a mirror in the hallway and looked at my face. There was an angry red mark across my face in the shape of her hand.

My face didn't hurt, though. I have a rare nerve condition that I can barely pronounce. Syringomyelia. The doctors tell me it's caused by a type of fluid that fills part of my spinal cord. It stops me from feeling a lot of pain, especially in my hands and shoulders and arms. Some people have it much worse and feel nothing. Me? Cuts and burns are just dull aches, enough to know something is wrong. Useful for a goalie.

But I still hadn't figured out how to keep the other stuff from hurting. Like being called fat. And like having a father in prison for stealing money from his television church ministry.

The rest of my Sunday was miserable.

Six

Al Handley, our assistant coach, sat down beside me in the dressing room. It was Monday afternoon, just before the final tryout practice. Today was the day that the coaches would make the last team cuts. Most of the other guys were already on the ice, so Al and I had the corner of the dressing room to ourselves.

Al is also the goalie coach. He's the only person I want to talk to before games.

Al used to be a goaltender himself. His age is hard to guess. Somewhere between fifty and seventy. He's tall and cigarette thin. He has washed out blue eyes, a long nose, and grooved wrinkles that run lengthwise down his face. And his voice is hardly more than a hoarse whisper.

"Gump," he said, "did I ever tell you about the time that Punch Imlach started talking about dumb players and dumb moves?"

I shook my head no. I knew who Punch Imlach was—

a famous NHL coach. Punch had taken the Toronto Maple Leafs to the Stanley Cup in the 1960s.

Maybe Al had played for Punch, maybe not. Al liked to make up stories. But I didn't mind. Because of Al, I was learning a lot about the history of the NHL. That's why I knew who Punch Imlach was. The other thing about Al was that he just took a guy for the way he was. No questions asked. No mean remarks about fat or fathers. Al was the closest to a friend I had on this team.

"It was in the dressing room after a game. Punch Imlach was in a bad mood that day," Al said. His voice started warming up the way it did when he told stories. "One of the defensemen had made a stupid move that cost us the game. Punch started shouting. 'I want to know how many dumb people I need to worry about for the rest of the season!' he yelled. 'Stand up so I can see who you are!'"

Al chuckled. "Punch stared at all of us, just waiting for someone to stand, so he could yell some more. After about a minute, I stood."

"*You* stood, Al?"

"Yup. Punch nearly had a heart attack. He looked at me and said, 'Al, you never struck me as dumb.' 'Yes, Coach,' I told him, 'but you looked real lonely standing up there all by yourself.'"

I laughed with Al.

"I got fined twenty-five dollars and suspended for one game," Al finished. "Back then, twenty-five dollars was a lot of money."

"Thanks for the story, Al."

"You looked like you could use some cheering up. I just wanted you to know that it's important to have fun playing hockey."

"You got it," I said. I almost meant it.

"Of course," he said, "Coach Mead also wants me to have a little chat with you."

"Oh?"

"Coach wants to know why Eddie jumped on you during the exhibition game. Eddie's probably going to make the team today. We'd like to straighten this out early."

I thought for a second. I wondered if Lauren was going to tell the coaches about the Ex-Lax. If she did, she'd tell them it was my idea. Maybe now was the time to blame someone else, before I got blamed.

I thought about it more. Al watched my face as I thought.

Maybe my code of honor was stupid. But I decided I wasn't going to squeal on any of my teammates. Not even on Eddie.

"I'd rather not talk about it," I said. "But there won't be another problem."

"That's fine with me," Al told me. "Just remember, if you ever need to talk, I'll listen."

"Thanks," I said.

He stood. "Well, practice is about to begin."

He grinned at me. "Think maybe today you'll actually do some work out there on the ice?"

"After all this time," I said, giving him my famous sour face look, "why start now?"

Seven

I skated onto the ice to practice, thinking about Al and what a great guy he was.

Two years earlier, when I joined the Spokane Chiefs, Al was the one who had given me my nickname, Gump the Grump. It wasn't because of the movie *Forrest Gump*. Instead, the "Gump" part came because Al remembered playing against one of the greatest goalies in the National Hockey League.

That goalie's name was Lorne John Worsely, but he was known as Gump Worsely. He was the NHL rookie of the year in 1952, and he played for more than twenty years. Al started calling me Gump because he says I play the same style. I know there is more to it than that, though. I've seen old photos of Gump Worsely. Just like me, Gump was short and wide. Gump Worsely even had the same kind of square face and the same kind of grumpy expression.

Most of the time I seem grumpy around the guys for

one simple reason. When it's time to play hockey, I don't talk. I think about the game and how I'm going to stop the puck from going into the net. The guys learned a long time ago that in the dressing room before a game, I want to be left alone. Practice was different. I still seemed grumpy, but I didn't work or think as hard then. I figured it was smarter to save energy for the games.

"Hey, Gump!" one of the guys said, breaking through my thoughts.

"Yeah?"

"Good to see you finally decided to show up for practice."

"You know me," I said. "It's my favorite thing."

"Yeah, and McDonald's has purple arches."

A couple more guys skated past me. They whacked my leg pads with their sticks. It's like saying hello to a goalie.

My face mask was tilted back on top of my head. I hid my smile. It felt good to be part of the team, even if I wasn't going to show it.

Coach Mead had us all skate a few laps. As we skated, he blew the whistle to speed us up. Then he blew it again to slow us down. Fast, slow. Fast, slow.

I skated at the same speed no matter what. Everyone knew that Gump the Grump saved his energy for when it really counted. That was part of being Gump the Grump.

I figured why waste good saves? I'd keep them for games. In practice, I would just stand in the net and cover the angles. If the puck hit me, fine. If it went in the net, oh well.

A reporter had once done a story on me. He'd written about the way I practice. He'd said I was probably the one goalie in the league who could get away with it. Just because I was too good in games to trade away. He'd pointed out that I had the highest goals-against average in practice and the lowest goals-against average in games.

Yes, I was one of the best in the league. Not a big deal. I was born with fast hands and I didn't feel pain.

What *was* a big deal was the fact that Lauren was almost as good. And she drew a bigger crowd. A lot of people wanted to cheer for her because she was a girl. And a lot wanted to cheer against her. I had a feeling she was going to get more ice time than I would.

I tried not to think about her as we changed to another drill. It didn't feel good to be hated by her. Especially for something that wasn't my fault.

After about ten minutes of the stop-and-start skating drill, Coach Mead broke the team into halves, sending us to opposite ends of the ice. Coach Mead went to the far end, away from me.

I pulled my goalie mask down over my face. I adjusted my pads to be comfortable. I stood in the net at my end as Al ran some passing and shooting drills. Players came down the ice, firing the puck at me. More pucks went into my net than stayed out. Oh well.

At the other end, Lauren Cross stopped everything they fired at her. She thought she had to prove herself every second in hockey.

I kept standing in the net, waiting for practice to end. I was bored. Just like I was during all normal, boring practices.

Except practice didn't stay boring much longer.

Halfway through, Eddie Dyer went nuts.

Eight

It started in a way that looked funny at first. We were doing a drill where the forward would start with the puck at center. He'd give a backhand pass to Al, who was standing at the blue line. The skater would charge toward the net, and Al would pass right into the forward's skates. The forward was supposed to kick the puck ahead onto his stick, then finish the breakaway* by taking the puck in and shooting at me.

When it was Eddie's turn, he made the mistake of stepping on the puck as he tried to kick it ahead. His foot slipped on the puck and shot out behind him. He landed on his nose and slid along the ice. The guys cracked up laughing.

Eddie didn't think it was funny.

He rolled over and stood. Then, without warning, he lifted his stick, gripped it with both hands above his head, and charged ahead. Eddie aimed straight at a left winger named Jeff Warner, our team captain.

For a couple seconds, Jeff thought Eddie was joking around. But Eddie kept roaring and kept charging. Jeff took a couple steps sideways.

Eddie still came after him.

Jeff decided skating away was smarter than staying. Jeff took off in my direction.

Eddie chased him.

Jeff skated behind the net.

Eddie chased him.

Jeff skated in front of me.

Eddie followed him around.

Jeff made another circle.

Eddie kept roaring, stick still above his head.

Everyone else at practice stared.

Finally, when Jeff made it around the net for the fourth time, Eddie stopped in front. I saw rage in Eddie's eyes, like he was a crazy man. I decided it would be a good time to leave.

Eddie didn't even notice me, even though I was three feet in front of him. He brought his stick down, trying to hit Jeff.

The stick splintered on the crossbar of the net. Had I left a second later, the stick would have split my helmet.

Eddie took another swing, bringing his stick down like an ax.

It splintered more.

Jeff skated away from the net.

Eddie didn't chase him. He stood where he was, yelling his anger and chopping at the top of the net again and again until his stick snapped. Even then, Eddie kept going. Wham! Wham! Wham!

By the time Al and Coach Mead dragged him away from the net, there was only about two feet of hockey stick, jagged and split at the end, left in Eddie's hands.

He didn't make the team.

Nine

Nobody really missed Eddie after he was cut from the team at the end of that practice. In fact, my guess was that a lot of the guys were relieved. Eddie was nothing but muscles and pimples. No brains. No class.

Jeff Warner said exactly that four road games later.

"Eddie Dyer was a jerk," Jeff said, raising his voice to be heard above the hum of the tires. "All muscle. No brains. And I'm not saying that just because he chased me. There were plenty of other times during tryouts that he did stupid things."

We were on the bus, headed back to Spokane from a trip that had taken us through Alberta and Saskatchewan. Over the last four days, we had played the Regina Blades, the Swift Current Broncos, the Medicine Hat Tigers, and finally, the Lethbridge Hurricanes. I'd been in the net for a win and a tie. Lauren had played one win and one loss. Which sounded good for me, except her average goals-against was lower than mine. And the fans loved her. I was beginning to wonder if I would get traded to another team.

My mind was on the goals that had been scored against me, so I only half listened to Jeff.

There were four of us sitting near the front of the bus. Assistant Coach Al Handley slouched in a seat on the other side of the aisle. Jeff Warner sat beside him at the window. With his blond hair, he looked more like a skier than a hockey player. Robert Zotski, a red-headed defenseman sat beside me. And I leaned against the other window.

"Yeah," Zotski said. "Not making the team last year really got to Eddie. He wasn't much of a player, so he worked on his body building. It was like the more muscle he put on, the meaner he got."

I kept staring out the window, thinking about stopping pucks. I didn't see much except stars. It had been a night game against the Hurricanes, and we were traveling home through the dark.

Zotski elbowed me. "Ain't that right, Gump? Last season's tryouts Eddie was an okay guy. There was no way he would have tried choking you like he did. This year? He was nuts! Remember the dumb penalties he took during the exhibition games? Running people into the boards. Chopping them with his stick. If Coach Mead had let him on the team, he might have really hurt someone."

I shrugged. "Probably. The guy was starting to look like a gorilla."

"Hey!" Jeff Warner said with a grin. "Check it out.

Gump spoke more than three words at once!"

"I'm surprised you can count to more than three," I told him. "You sure you didn't have help from Al?"

"Hah, hah," Jeff said.

Al just stretched and chuckled.

The bus began to slow down as we reached a section of highway with street lights.

"The border," Zotski said. He stood and looked through the front window of the bus. "Good news. Only a few cars ahead of us."

That was one thing about going back into Washington from Canada. Going through customs could take anywhere from five minutes to an hour, depending on traffic.

"Al," Jeff said, "enough about Eddie Dyer. Got any stories we haven't heard before?"

Al gave us a fox grin. "How about my first game in the net against Hull?"

"Right," Jeff said, rolling his eyeballs and snorting with disbelief. "You played against Brett Hull. Was Hull wearing diapers then?"

"Tell him, Gump," Al said. "At least *you* know something about the history of the game."

"Not Brett Hull," I told Jeff. "Bobby Hull, Brett's dad. Played for the Chicago Black Hawks until he got offered a couple million to play for the Winnipeg Jets when the Jets were a part of the World Hockey Association."

I paused, remembering something. "Unless Al is talking about Dennis Hull, Brett's uncle."

"It was Bobby," Al said. "One of the first players in the NHL to use the slap shot."

"Huh?" Jeff said. "First? Didn't they always have slap shots?"

"Tell him more, Gump," Al said in his raspy old-man's voice.

The bus moved forward slowly, then stopped again. I glanced out the window. Only one car left between us and the border.

"It was in the sixties, Jeff," I explained, secretly proud that Al expected me to know. "Slap shots were new to the game. That was back when goaltenders didn't wear face masks."

"Back when you didn't need a face mask," Al said. "Back before the curved hockey stick. But let me tell you, when Hull showed players what slap shots and curved sticks could do, everything changed. It made life some kind of tough on us goalies. We never knew where the puck would go. Half the time I don't think Hull had any idea either. And that's how he managed to bang one off my skull."

We leaned forward to listen better. Al told great stories, even if they might not be true.

"See, it was a night in Chicago . . ." Al began.

He stopped as the bus driver opened the door. Two customs guys stepped onto the bus.

"Who's in charge?" one of the officers asked. He had a crew cut and a huge belly.

Coach Mead stood, wearing his team jacket. Coach

Mead was a big man. He had a crew cut too. But no belly. "I am."

"We want to search the hockey equipment," the customs guy said. "All of it."

All of the talking on the bus stopped.

"You're kidding, right?" Coach Mead said. "You border guys have never checked us before."

"We're not kidding," the customs guy said. His face looked serious.

"That could take hours," Coach Mead said. "These guys have been on the road for four days. They're beat up and dog tired. Besides, they're junior hockey players. What have they got that you're interested in?"

"Telling us how to do our job is not smart," the other guy said. "We can take this entire bus apart if we want."

Coach Mead's expression tightened. We recognized the look and knew he was angry. But Coach Mead was too smart to push the guys in uniform.

"Park the bus," Coach Mead said to the driver. "You can probably grab a cup of coffee or something while you wait."

A few minutes later, the customs guys started pulling duffel bags out of the luggage space of the bus.

Coach Mead was right about one thing. We were all beat up and tired. But Coach Mead was wrong about something else.

The search didn't take hours. It took less than fifteen minutes. Which was how long it took for them to find illegal steroids in Lauren Cross's equipment.

Ten

"**H**ow are you feeling?" Al asked me. His raspy voice was down to a whisper. He knew I didn't enjoy much talk before games. "You okay with the pressure?"

"What pressure?"

"What do you mean what pressure? Tonight's the first home game of the season. And there's been two days of headlines since they found all those steroids in Lauren's equipment at the border. Not only that, do you have any idea how many press passes the front office gave out today? I'll bet we get at least thirty reporters to the game tonight."

"Not much pressure if you don't read the newspapers," I said.

Near us in the dressing room, the other guys were joking around.

After he thought about that for a second, Al chuckled. "Good one, Gump. Where did you learn to be that smart?"

I could have told him I had learned it last summer,

when my father was on trial back in Vancouver for stealing money from old ladies and orphans. I could have told him I learned that if you didn't read the papers or watch the news on television, you wouldn't know what people were saying. But I didn't tell Al any of that. There was no sense in taking the crooked smile off Al's face. I just shrugged.

"That reminds me," Al said, "did I ever tell you about the time that—"

"Guys! Guys! Guys!" Jeff Warner shouted at the front of the dressing room. "Listen up!"

We stopped what we were doing. It was ten minutes before the game. We had already done our warm-up skate. So we were sitting and resting.

I had skated hard during warm-ups, and sweat was rolling down my face. I wiped my face with a towel as I listened to Jeff.

"Thank you," Jeff said in a quieter voice. As captain, he was used to talking to the entire team.

"They're going to do the Bambi trick on the new goalie tonight," Al whispered in my ear. "This will be great. Right, Gump?"

"Sure, Al. Real fun."

Jeff looked all around the room. He kept a big grin on his face.

"Big game tonight, boys," Jeff said. "Keep in mind that we'll be in first place if we beat the Thunderbirds. That would be a nice place to be this early in the season."

"Warner, you meatball," Robert Zotski yelled from his corner of the dressing room. "Give it a rest!

Coach Mead gives the pep talks. And he does them a lot better than you."

Coach Mead looked up from his clipboard and smiled. Everyone—except the new goalie—knew Zotski and Warner were best friends.

Jeff looked over at the new guy to our team, the goalie brought in to replace Lauren Cross. "Ignore Zotski," Jeff told the new goalie. "Everyone else does."

The new goalie gave him a nervous grin. His name was Luke Schuman. He was tall and gangly. He had stringy brown hair down to his shoulders. He was younger than most of us and had only joined the team the day before. I remembered being nervous when I had first signed on too.

"Anyway guys," Jeff said, "this is also a big game for another reason. You've all met Luke. And you all know this will be his first game in the WHL."

Luke's nervous grin got bigger. Rookies were always a little scared to be thrown onto a team. For Luke, it must have been worse than usual because of why he had been brought in. People couldn't believe Lauren had been caught with illegal steroids in her hockey equipment. She was gone from the WHL as fast as she had arrived, and with as many headlines. Luke was here to replace her.

"And guys," Jeff said, "it's a real special night for Luke for another reason."

"This is going to be good," Al whispered in my ear. "Remember when we did this to you?"

Yes, I remembered. I hung my head for poor Luke. If

it happened to him like it had happened to me, he wouldn't know what hit him.

"Yes," Jeff said, "Luke's whole family is here to see his first WHL game."

"All right!" one of the guys said. "Way to go Luke!"

A few other guys whistled. All of them knew what was happening. They were doing their best to make the prank work.

"Quiet!" Jeff shouted at them. He turned to Luke. "Hey, bud. It's a big night for you. We'd like you to lead the team onto the ice. You know, when the announcer is calling out the players' names."

"Cool," Luke said. Usually the starting goaltender led the team onto the ice. "That's real nice of you guys."

"Well, your family is here. It's an honor we'd like them to share with you," Jeff said. "And we just want you to know you're part of the team."

I hung my head lower. Poor Luke.

"Now listen close," Jeff told Luke. "Since it's a big game tonight, we need you to set the tone. Charge out onto the ice like you're leading an army. Skate out there hard and pump up the entire team!"

Luke nodded. The look on his face said there was no way he would dream of letting us down.

Poor Luke.

Jeff clapped his hands together once. "Enough said. Let's get ready. And let's go get them."

Five minutes later, the team lined up to leave the dressing room. In the hallway beneath the stands of the arena, we walked on the rubber matting that protected our skate blades from the concrete beneath. Luke was at the front of the line, with Jeff right behind him, and me following Jeff.

As we walked, Jeff half-turned and grinned at all of us. Luke, of course, didn't see that. Poor Luke.

We turned from the hallway toward the ice, walking through a narrow corridor. There was a gate in the boards. An arena employee opened the gate to let us onto the ice.

"And now," the announcer said over the loudspeakers, "the Spokane Chiefs!"

The crowd roared and cheered.

"Okay, Luke!" Jeff shouted. "We'll be right behind you. Charge out there hard!"

Luke jumped onto the ice and pushed off to take his first step.

He fell flat on his face.

Jeff stayed where he was and kept the rest of us from going onto the ice to join Luke. There he was, all by himself, in front of thousands of people. In front of his family and friends who had come to see his first WHL game. And he was flat on his face.

Luke got to his skates. It wasn't easy in that heavy goalie equipment. He took another step.

He fell flat on his face again.

In the movie *Bambi,* there's a part where Bambi tries to walk on ice and his feet keep going out from under him. That's what Luke looked like over the next minute. Every time he stood and took a step, he fell. Up, down. Up, down. Bam, bam, bam.

Finally, Jeff took pity on him and led the rest of us onto the ice.

As the other players laughed and chuckled, I skated to Luke and helped him stand.

"Oh man!" he said. He didn't know whether to laugh or cry. "Oh man! What's happening?"

"Sorry, bud," I told him. "They put Scotch tape along the bottoms of your skate blades. Lift one of your skates, and I'll peel it off."

One skate at a time, I helped him.

Guys skated all around us as they did their final laps to warm up before the game started. They slapped him on the back and welcomed him to the team.

"If it makes you feel better," I said. "They do this to most rookies. Now you're really part of the team."

He managed to give me a shaky grin. Then he pushed away and skated. The crowd cheered him.

As for me, I headed toward the net. With Lauren Cross gone, it was all mine again. For better or for worse.

Eleven

The referee dropped the puck to start the game. Whistling and cheering filled the air. I stared ahead and ignored the fans. What I saw instead were ten skaters on center ice. Five in our uniforms. Five in Seattle Thunderbirds uniforms.

Jeff Warner, at center, pulled the puck back to Mick Williams, one of our defensemen. Mick fired the puck into the Seattle end, and our forwards chased after it.

I watched and waited as the ten skaters moved in a swirling pattern across the ice. I might have looked relaxed as I stood between the goal posts in our end. But I wasn't. I had just under sixty minutes of playing time ahead of me. Most games I faced thirty to forty shots. Altogether those shots might add up to two minutes of making saves. Two minutes of facing hard rubber that could hit me from any angle at over 100 miles an hour. Two minutes of standing up to guys who might skate over me on blades as sharp as razors. In other words, somewhere during the next fifty-nine minutes, I would face two minutes of sheer terror.

And it would all start with the first shot.

For most goalies, that first shot is the biggest save of the game. If you don't stop the first shot, you'll be afraid of every shot for the rest of the game.

I always hope the first shot happens right away. It's strange, in a way, to wish for that. But until I make the first save, I'm as jittery as a cat in a room with five dogs. And, just like that cat, I'm on my toes and watching real close, even with the puck in the other end.

So I watched as our forwards attacked the Seattle defensemen and tried to force them to cough up the puck.

A minute later, Mick, playing the left side on defense at their blue line, made a big mistake. I saw it clearly. And so did all the fans in the ice arena.

The Thunderbirds winger had picked up the puck along the boards, halfway to their blue line. Mick should have played it safe and started skating backward. Instead, he took a chance and dashed toward the winger. Mick was gambling, hoping to knock the puck back toward the Thunderbirds' net.

It didn't work.

The Thunderbirds winger saw him early and chipped the puck off the boards and past Mick. He ducked Mick's body check* and chased after the puck. That left Mick deep in the Thunderbirds' end, with no way to turn around in time to catch up to the Thunderbirds winger.

Worse, two of their forwards were already at full speed, breaking out of the Thunderbirds' end. And all of our forwards were still deep in the Thunderbirds' zone. That meant all three of Seattle's first-line forwards were headed my way with the puck. Only one of our defensemen stood between them and me.

Noise grew, a noise I barely heard. I quickly felt behind me for the right goal post. That let me keep my eyes on the puck and still know exactly where I was in the net. I shifted my eyes from the puck to the skaters and back to the puck again. They were all across the center line, with our forwards too far away to catch up.

I drifted ahead. Just a little. Normally, a good move is to come out of the net and challenge the shooter. It cuts down on the angles open to him. But on a three-against-one breakaway, I didn't expect a shot. Instead, they would pass the puck around and move in close.

Now they were at the blue line. I forced myself to stay calm, relaxed. It's the only way a goalie can react quickly. If you squeeze your muscles tight with worry, you can't flop or dive nearly as fast.

The forward in the center kept the puck. The Thunderbird on the right slowed down and cut in behind him. The Thunderbird on the left cut around the outside, skating hard. That put our defenseman in a bad position. If he stayed with the puck, the outside guy would be open for a pass. But if he went for the outside guy, it opened up the middle for the other two skaters.

I stayed loose, legs bent at the knees, stick on the ice. The important thing was to let them make the first move.

Our defenseman waited as long as he could, then edged over to guard against the pass to the outside. Their center reacted by breaking hard the other way. I shifted to cover the angle against him.

Now they were halfway between me and the blue line. Whatever happened would happen in the next few heartbeats.

Our defenseman cut back to the middle to take the puck carrier. For a split second, with his legs crossing over, the defenseman left an unguarded gap. Their center fed the puck straight across to the skater on the far left.

I turned to cut down that angle. But I didn't make much of a turn. The biggest mistake I could make would be moving my feet. A goalie has to be set. When his feet are moving, he leaves openings.

The winger brought his stick back to slap a shot. I almost fell to block it, but something in my mind screamed against it. It must have been something in the way the winger set up his shoulders. Something I could not explain but felt from watching thousands and thousands of slap shots. *He was going to fake the shot. I knew it. And there was still the third skater, wide open behind the play.*

I dipped my shoulder like I was actually falling for the fake shot. This was the crucial moment. If he did shoot, I was dead.

He saw my move and decided I was starting to dive to block the shot. He fell for my fake. He spun the puck backward to his teammate in the middle. At the same time, I was pulling myself back from the dive and setting up square. Just as the shooter committed himself, I pushed straight ahead. By moving closer to him, I took away almost all of the net.

His stick whipped down. Crack!

I didn't have time to react. That's how close he was. But I didn't need to react. I had outsmarted him. Where I was, all I needed to do was hold my ground. The puck hit the outside of my leg pad and dropped, just to my side.

Now I needed to move, and I needed to move fast.

I flopped, diving on the puck to cover it before the center or the winger could whack in a rebound. I smothered the puck with my catching glove.

Big save! The crowd roared.

But it wasn't over yet.

Their center, close in on the puck, brought his stick down, trying to knock the puck from my glove. I was on my knees, twisted sideways, pulling the puck in toward me. He only caught a piece of my glove, but it was enough.

He knocked the puck loose. *It wobbled backward toward the open net.*

Our defenseman rammed him, pushing him away from me. That gave me room. Still on my knees, with my knees facing toward the other net, I stretched backward. I managed to lean behind me and get my glove on the puck again.

That should have ended the play.

Except the shooter had a clear run. Just as the referee was blowing the whistle, the shooter skated in. He stepped on my stick and fell on top of me. I was in a bad position for that kind of hit. On my knees, twisted sideways, and reaching backward. His total weight fell on top of me.

I felt a dull pain in my left thigh. He'd stretched me backward as far as I could go.

Seconds later, our guys were there, pulling him off me and shouting at him.

I relaxed. The ref had blown the whistle. The puck was in my glove. I'd made a big, big save.

The guys cleared out in front of me.

I stood.

At least, I tried to stand.

The dull pain was still in my thigh. I wobbled to my feet. I fell. I tried to get to my feet again. I fell.

This wasn't good. I wasn't falling because of a Bambi prank. There was no tape on my skate blades. I was falling because something was wrong in the muscles of my left thigh. There have been times that I've been cut and not felt anything. For me to even feel a dull pain, there had to be something terribly wrong.

On my third try to get to my feet, I fell and decided it would be smarter to lay on the ice until they took me away.

Twelve

It was afternoon the day after the game when Lauren Cross walked into my hospital room. I hadn't seen her since the drugs had been found in her equipment. But I'd heard that a lawyer had arranged bail and that Lauren hadn't actually had to spend any time in jail. A trial was coming up next month. Until then, she was free.

For a few seconds, we just stared at each other. Me, the nearly fat guy in ugly green hospital pajamas on a lumpy bed in a dull white room. Her, in jeans, T-shirt, and black leather jacket, with her flashing eyes, strangely pretty face, and thick, long red hair.

"Come to tell me how happy you are about my injury?" I asked. "Or are you going to start throwing things at me again?"

"I want to do both," she said. "But I won't."

She walked to the chair near my bed. She sat down without asking me if it was okay. Which it was. Much as she hated me, and much as I hated admitting it to myself, something about her made my heart beat faster.

"So . . ." she said.

"So . . ." I said.

I waited for her to speak. I guessed she had a reason for visiting me. But, like in goaltending, I figured it was better to let her make the first move.

"Your quad," she said, pointing at the metal brace on my left leg. "I heard it was your quadricep muscle."

"Yeah," I said. "I have to keep it still so it can heal. The muscle was torn. But I should be back on the ice in a month."

"Oh. The newspaper said you could be out for the rest of the season."

"Never believe what Steve Haliburton writes," I told her. "If that reporter doesn't get a good quote, he makes one up."

She raised her eyebrows, like she didn't believe me. I pointed at the paper on the table near my bed. "Look through the article," I said. "You'll read the part where I say how much it hurt to have my muscle torn up."

"And?" She didn't bother reaching for the paper.

"As they were taking me to the hospital last night, he caught up to us in the parking lot. All I said to him was the same thing I always say to the reporters, no matter what they ask."

"Which is?"

"We played a hard game. Although we lost, we gave it our best shot. And win or lose, this is a team game. A couple of bounces our way instead of theirs, and it might have been a different game tonight."

"That's all you ever say?"

I grinned at her. "Unless we win. Then I tell the reporters something different."

"Yeah?" She actually smiled. "Like what?"

"We played a hard game. Although we won, it took our best shot. And win or lose, this is a team game. A couple of bounces their way instead of ours, and it might have been a different game tonight."

"If I were a reporter," she said, "I'd stop asking you questions."

I grinned again. "Exactly."

She picked up the newspaper to check the part where Steve Haliburton had me saying something I'd never said. She began to read out loud. "'I can't believe how much it hurt,' said goalie Joseph Larken. 'The guy ran me over and it felt like my muscle was torn in two.'"

She frowned. "You didn't say that?"

"No." And I never would. Because I have the nerve disorder called Syringomyelia. People who have it are always in danger. Imagine if you couldn't feel pain. If you stepped on something and cut your foot, you might bleed to death before you noticed. Or if you leaned your hand against something hot, you'd burn yourself and not know it until you smelled the roasting skin.

The doctors say that I have a mild form of this nerve condition and that I'll be okay if I'm careful. But it was still one of the reasons my mother didn't want me to be a goalie. She wondered why I would put myself in a position where I could get hurt. I wondered why she didn't understand that I needed to prove I was normal. Of course, my mother also wanted me to be a preacher. Like my father. Fat chance of that.

"But why do you have this thing about reporters?" she asked.

"Long story," I told her, thinking of the summer before and the nightmare of news stories about my father. "You don't want to be bored with it."

"And if I did?" She was smiling.

"You didn't stop by to wish me well," I said. Time to change the subject. "You probably had another reason."

That took the smile off her face, as if I had reminded her of why she hated me.

"You're going to help me get back on the team," she said, her lips suddenly tight with anger. "Whether you want to or not."

"Oh?"

"I didn't stash those steroids in my equipment," she said. "Someone else did. Someone who wanted me to get caught."

"Oh?"

"I've been thinking about it all week. Why did those customs guys stop the bus and start searching? Someone had to have called and alerted them to look for drugs. The same someone who put the drugs in my stuff."

"Oh?"

"I need someone on the team to help me by looking into it for me. I can't. So I decided it's going to be you."

"It won't be me," I said.

"Two reasons," she said, not listening to me. "One, you can't play for a while anyway."

"Watch my lips," I said. "It . . . won't . . . be . . . me."

"And the second reason is even simpler. If you don't help, I'm going to call Steve Haliburton at the newspaper. I'll tell him a great theory. That you were the one who planted those drugs. That you were the one who called the customs guys."

"Why would Haliburton believe you?" I said.

"Because I'll also tell him about the stuff you put in my hot chocolate. Even though Eddie Dyer didn't make the team, I still have him as witness to that. It will look like once you couldn't get me to quit with the Ex-Lax trick, you went even further."

I crossed my arms. I could feel stubbornness growing inside me, becoming a big, hard boulder.

"Once that story hits the papers," she said, "you're going to look like a first-class jerk. People might even start to believe you were the one who planted the steroids in my equipment."

"Do what you want," I said, arms still crossed. "I'm not letting you blackmail me into helping."

"We'll see," she said, her voice as stubborn as mine.

"Besides," I went on, "what makes you so sure it wasn't me?"

"Because," she said, "it was our assistant coach. Al Handley."

Thirteen

Why don't you take a hike," I said, taking a deep breath. "Take a long walk off a short pier, play in traffic, jump from an airplane without a 'chute. Anything. I don't care. As long as it is away from this room. I'm finished talking with you."

"Let me guess," she said, her face turning red at the anger in my voice. "Al Handley's your hero? You don't dare think anything bad about him?"

I put a cold smile on my face and left it there. I didn't say a word.

"Al's everybody's hero," she said. "Nice guy, tells great stories, hangs out, and is a buddy when you need him. Right?"

I just gave her the brick wall of my cold smile.

She stood up and put her face within inches of mine. "Al the hero is the same person who is selling steroids," she said, her voice a hiss.

My smile didn't change.

"Think about Eddie Dyer. Big muscles in one season. Huge, greasy pimples. Loses his temper easily at little things and goes totally nuts. Those are all the classic things that happen to people on steroids."

I folded my arms. I turned my eyes to hers. I kept smiling.

"How do I know, you might ask?" She straightened and backed away from me. She was clenching her fists as if she were trying not to hit me. It felt good, making her mad without saying a word.

"Because I followed Al this week," she said. "Three times he went to the gym where Eddie works out. He hung around with Eddie for a half hour each time. Later on, I asked other weightlifters about Eddie. Everyone there knows Eddie has been taking steroids. Where's he getting them from? Al."

I kept smiling. If she thought I was going to say a single word, she was wrong.

"Al," she said. "I've gone through it in my mind again and again. He's the only one who ever touches my equipment. He's the only one I ever left it with. I thought he was being a gentleman, helping me get it on and off the bus back in Lethbridge. But no, he was planting drugs in my duffel bag."

I nearly slipped up. I nearly opened my mouth and asked why Al would do something like that. I nearly asked why Al—if he were selling drugs—would need to get Lauren in trouble. But I kept smiling. A cold, cold smile.

"You are a pig-headed jerk," she said. She kicked

59

the chair. "Listen to me! Al hated seeing a girl play hockey. Just like you. Except he went way further. He didn't put Ex-Lax in my hot chocolate. He tried to get me put in jail."

Smile. Smile. Smile. That's all Lauren was going to get from me.

"Fine," she said.

I knew my smile was working when she said that. The only time women say "fine" is when it isn't. I knew that from all the times I had smiled and kept my mouth shut in arguments about my father with my mother.

"Fine," she repeated. "As soon as I leave this room, I'm calling Steve Haliburton at the newspaper. Remember? The Steve Haliburton who makes up quotes. We'll see what he does when I tell him what you did to get me off the ice. We'll see what he does when I tell him you went as far as putting drugs in my duffel bag."

Smile. Smile. Smile. Hah. Hah. Hah. She wasn't getting to me at all.

Lauren marched to the door. At the doorway, she stopped and turned around. She stared at me for a few moments. Rage left her face.

"You'll stop smiling soon enough," she said, suddenly calm. "Imagine what it will be like when people start talking about this. They'll think you're just like your father. Don't think I haven't heard all about him. From everyone."

She took a step through the doorway.

"Wait," I said.

She turned back to me.

"I detest you," I said. I remembered what people had said about my father, how he was dishonest. I didn't want them to say the same about Al. Dad deserved it. Al didn't. I didn't care much about what people said about me, but I wasn't going to let it happen to Al. "Very much. But I'll help."

"I guess we're even," she said. "I detest you too."

"Don't think I'm helping because I'm afraid that you'll go to Steve Haliburton. I don't care what the newspapers say."

"Right," she said. Scorn filled her face. "That's why you always tell them the same thing, no matter what they ask you."

I ignored that. I had to. It was too close to the truth.

"I'm only going to help you long enough to prove you're wrong about Al," I said. "Then I hope I never see you again."

Fourteen

Say you really admired someone. Say you admired that someone as much as you would admire your dad—if you had a dad worth admiring. Then say someone else said some bad things about that someone. You probably wouldn't be able to stop thinking about it.

I sure couldn't.

Especially since Al was a big part of my hockey life.

The next Saturday night we had a game against the Red Deer Rebels.

Although my leg was still in the brace, I joined the team in the dressing room. The guys shook their heads at my bad luck. They all wished me well. Then they went back to their conversations and to getting ready for the game.

I took a spot on the bench beside Luke Schuman, who was just starting to strap on his leg pads. I propped my leg on a chair and sat back to watch the activities of the dressing room.

Mainly, I watched Al. As always, he had a big grin on his face. As always, he was talking to one of the players. If Al wasn't telling a story, he was giving advice. And it was usually good advice.

I didn't want to believe what Lauren had said about him.

I started to toss thoughts around. *If Al were into steroids, then Cindy Crawford was going to call and ask me to marry her. No, if Al were into steroids, I would be able to spit diamonds. No, if Al were into steroids . . .*

"Gump." Luke Schuman interrupted my thoughts.

"Yeah?"

"Al said you're the best goalie around. He said I should talk to you if I got nervous about starting in the net tonight."

I felt guilty. Here I was, trying to convince myself to not believe something bad about Al, and he'd said nice things about me.

"I'm too dumb to get nervous," I said. "That's all."

"Al said you're the smartest goalie he's ever coached."

"Oh," I said, feeling more guilty. I tried to change the subject. "Are you nervous about tonight's game?"

"I want to throw up," Luke said. His long skinny face was shiny with sweat.

"That could be a good thing," I said. "Ever heard of Glenn Hall?"

"I think so." By the expression on Luke's face, I could see he had not.

"An NHL Hall of Famer," I explained, remembering what Al had once told me. "He played in the NHL from

1952 to 1971. He was so scared, he threw up in a bucket before every game. People said his bucket should be in the Hall of Fame too. He had ulcers and everything. But he was good. Real good."

"Why would anyone play if he were that scared?"

I grinned. "Why are you playing if you're scared?"

A smile reached his eyes. "Good point."

"Luke," I said. "You want some advice?"

He swallowed and nodded at the same time. His chin bobbed along with his Adam's apple.

"First of all," I said, "this isn't coming from me. It's from Al. He's been a big help ever since I got to the team."

Why was everything coming back to Al? I realized that it would kill me to find out I couldn't trust Al. *First my dad. Then Al . . .*

"Great goalies all do one thing," I said quickly, trying to get my mind off of my worries. "They don't fold under pressure. Bad goalies? They try to look good."

I felt like a wise old man, talking to this rookie. It didn't feel bad.

"Yeah," I said. "Bad goalies think this game is about diving or doing the splits or reaching to stop the impossible shots. No way. The biggest thing is to stop all the shots you should. Cover the angles, play safe, and don't let any bad goals in. It looks boring. Almost like you're standing there doing nothing. But great goalies know where to stand."

"That's what Al said about you."

Al again. I was going to do everything in my power to prove Lauren wrong.

"Actually, that's what Al taught me," I said. "The whole thing is to make the shooter beat you with a good move or a good shot. See, everyone in this league knows that I go down in a butterfly all the time. It's true. But look at the butterfly style. Your stick guards the hole between your knees as you drop. Your leg pads fill either side to both posts. All you leave them is the few inches at the top of the net."

Luke nodded, soaking it up like I always soaked it up from Al.

"Well," I said, "under pressure, hitting the top of the net is a tough shot. I mean, who's more nervous in a close game? You or the shooter who thinks it's his chance to be a hero? As the goalie, if you stay calm and control your emotions and concentrate on the game instead of on winning or losing, you'll be one of the great ones."

Luke grinned. "Al was right. You are a big help."

I don't know if it was Al's advice that I passed on, or if it was Luke deciding he could be a good goalie instead of a nervous rookie, but things went well that night.

We won 5–2, and Luke stopped thirty-five shots.

The only bad part about the entire evening was what happened after the game—when I saw Al in the parking lot long after the crowd and most of the team had gone home.

Fifteen

My car is a Volkswagen. Not a new one. It's not only called a Beetle, it also looks like one. It's almost round, and it has buggy eyes for headlights. It is over twenty years old and drives and sounds like it's fifty.

I sat in it with my window open. I was slouched down. My car was in deep shadow, just past the circle of white from a street light. Even though the parking lot was almost empty, I was pretty sure I was hard to see in the darkness of my car.

Before the game, I had parked near Al's car, an old black Corvette. It stood beneath the light. Although it's an older model, it looks good. Al always said that, except for his wife's wedding ring, his 'Vette was the only fancy thing in his life.

I stared at his car, waiting and feeling very stupid. I was only waiting because I couldn't think of anything better to do. Like, was I going to ask Al if he was part of this steroids thing? My plan was to follow him around for a few days, long enough to prove to Lauren that she was totally wrong.

Al's echoing footsteps reached me above the faraway sounds of traffic. Al wore cowboy boots. Old, beat-up cowboy boots. With his kind of half-limping walk from a knee injury, we always knew when it was Al coming down the hallway.

I was ready in case Al noticed me. I would tell him I was waiting to ask him a question. Then I would. I would ask him if he wanted me to work with Luke while I was healing from my injury.

But Al didn't see me.

He walked to his car. As he fumbled in his pocket for keys, I saw movement far past the Corvette. A moving shadow. From a car. It didn't have its headlights on.

Something about the way it moved slowly and quietly and almost invisibly gave me prickles of fear. I thought of movies where the bad guys tried to run over the good guys. And sometimes actually hit them.

Should I shout something to Al?

Al heard something though. He turned around. And waited.

So did I.

The car got closer and slid into the light beside Al's Corvette. The car was a Mustang. Red. I knew that car. It belonged to Eddie Dyer.

I slid down even farther in my car seat. I peeked over the edge of my door. I listened hard.

The Mustang door opened and closed, a clear sound above the hard beating of my heart. Eddie stepped toward Al. Their voices reached me, but not clearly enough to hear what either of them said.

I watched the same way I watch a shooter when he has the puck and is cruising toward the net like a nasty shark.

Al handed Eddie an envelope. Eddie looked into it and grinned his mean grin. He tucked the envelope into his back pocket.

Eddie backed away, toward his Mustang.

Al stood, keys still in his hand as Eddie began to open his car door.

Al called out to him: "Ten o'clock. Don't forget. Ten o'clock. That's tomorrow. Not Monday or yesterday. Tomorrow."

Eddie saluted Al, then slipped into his car. The Mustang's headlights snapped on. Eddie drove away, squealing his tires.

Al watched the Mustang until the red taillights turned around the side of the arena. Then Al shook his head, as if he were sad or tired. Al got into his own car and drove away quietly.

As for me, I stared at my steering wheel for a long time before I finally cranked up my old, beat-up little Beetle.

Sixteen

My Volkswagen Beetle is an automatic. They'd never been very popular because they sometimes popped out of gear if you bumped the gearshift. There aren't many automatics around. And even though I didn't have to use a clutch, it was still tough to drive with my left leg in a brace. The doctor said I'd have to wear it for a week or so to immobilize the muscle while it was healing.

I banged the steering wheel with my hands and shouted in anger at my bum leg . . . and because I was angry at Al and needed an excuse to yell.

Halfway out of the parking lot, I thought of something. I turned around and drove up to the side of the arena. I swung my legs out of the car and grabbed my crutches. I stood on my good leg and used the crutches to hobble to the side door. Then I banged on the door with a crutch until someone finally opened the door.

"George," I said. "Thanks."

The short, bald man in front of me grinned, showing

a gap between his front teeth. Beside him stood his son, Skids. George was carrying a mop. Down the hall, I saw his bucket.

"Gump," he said. He touched my crutches with the end of his mop handle. "So sad about your leg. Me and my boy, we been praying for you."

I must have looked puzzled. "You're a good kid," he said. "Me, a janitor most people don't see. You're the only one who remembers my name. Let me tell you, I sure appreciate that."

Skids nodded and grinned. He hung out with his father when George worked the night shift. Skids always came out to the parking lot when we were unloading the bus after road trips. He was about thirty years old but was always excited like a kid to help us. He was short and skinny. I'd heard stories about a car accident that had injured his brain. That's why people called him Skids.

I smiled, said thanks, and walked past them. That had been the first nice thing to happen to me all week.

The building was quiet and mostly dark. I heard a few players still in the dressing room at the end of the hall. But I limped to our trainer Johnny Kempstock's office, hoping he hadn't gone home yet. I relaxed when I saw that his door was open. Break number two.

As I got closer, Steve Haliburton stepped out of Johnny's office.

"Gump," Steve said to me. "What'd you think about the game?"

I knew how some reporters worked. They asked you a question like they were just making conversation. You might say something stupid because you didn't think it was an official interview. And then the next day, you'd see what you said in some article.

"We played a hard game," I said. "Although we won, it took our best shot. And win or lose, this is a team game. A couple of bounces their way instead of ours, and—"

"Yeah, yeah, yeah," he said. He waved his hand in disgust and walked away.

The third nice thing in less than two minutes. I had managed to make a reporter grumpy instead of the other way around. If things kept going like this, I wouldn't have any problems with Johnny.

I hobbled through the doorway. Johnny was at his desk, closing a drawer.

"Hey, Johnny," I said. "Can you help me?"

"Gump, for you, anything." Johnny was a college student. Short, like me. But a lot skinnier. Johnny was taking classes to be a physical therapist. He looked at his trainer's position as a good way to get practical experience.

Johnny grinned. "Is it your leg? Need some aspirin?"

"No," I said. "Information."

"This ought to be good," he said. "The famous Gump, actually showing interest in something besides goal-tending."

Was I really that bad? I put the question aside for later when I could stare at the ceiling and worry about life.

"Any chance you can let me look through your players' notebook?" I asked. It was a brown one. We players had learned to hate it because Johnny only took it out when he was going to work on us.

71

"My medical journal? Why?" he asked. His grin changed to a frown. "I just finished telling that no good reporter he wasn't going to get any information about players' injuries from me."

"I just need to know where one of the guys lives," I said. "He played a practical joke on me."

"I get it." His grin returned. "A practical joke. This team is full of practical jokers."

He shook his head as if we were all crazy. "Hockey players. You know Zotski is still hopping mad about his shoes."

Last week, someone had nailed Zotski's shoes to the floor beneath his bench. The rest of the team had cracked up as he yanked at them, getting madder and madder until he'd finally noticed the nails. Then he'd really started yelling.

I sat down as Johnny spun his chair around and dug into his filing cabinet. The smell of heat liniment and sweaty socks filled my nose.

He finally pulled out a notebook from deep inside.

"I'm an okay trainer," he said, "but I need a secretary."

I smiled and took the book. I started to leaf through the pages. I flipped through slowly. Each page had a player's name and a record of any medical problems and Johnny's treatments. I was relieved to see pages for players who had been cut. It's a good thing Johnny wasn't more organized.

I don't know why, but it seemed smart not to let Johnny know what I was looking for. It seemed smart not to let anyone know. So after I had taken a good look at the page for Eddie Dyer, I kept slowly flipping the pages. When I reached the N's, I shut the notebook and handed it back to Johnny.

"Thanks," I said, pushing myself to my feet. It took a while to get my crutches in place.

When I finally got to the hallway, Skids was waiting for me by himself.

"Got something for you," Skids said. He grinned, like a little kid looking up at his older brother. "Something to make your leg better."

I smiled. Skids spoke slowly as if too many thoughts confused him.

"The doctor told me I need physical therapy," I told him.

Skids shook his head and held his hand open. There was a small plastic bag with some pills. "I got a friend who gives me these. Muscle building pills. You can have these for free."

Muscle building pills?

He frowned. "Sorry, Gump. But my friend needs money if you want more."

Then he brightened. "Try them. They'll get you on the ice again fast."

Muscle building pills?

I nearly made a joke and asked him if he meant steroids. And then I nearly told him no. Until I realized something else.

So instead of saying no, I told him sure. And I stuffed the pills in my pocket.

Seventeen

W hose car?" Lauren asked, like there was nothing unusual about me picking her up at seven o'clock on a Sunday morning. "I thought you had a beat-up buggy-looking thing."

"My billets'," I said. "The DuPonts. I didn't think it would be smart to follow Eddie in my VW."

Lauren was already in the car on the passenger side, but I didn't look across at her. When I had called her late last night, I had still been mad at her for the things she'd said about me and my father.

"You didn't tell me much over the phone," she said. "Plus I was half asleep when you called. What exactly is going on?"

I put the car in gear and drove away from the curb. It was a gray Volvo station wagon. Very boring. Very invisible. No one would expect me to be in it.

"There are a couple of things." I realized I was also angry at Lauren for being right about Al. Almost like

I thought it was her fault that he was involved in all this.

"First," I said, "last night Al gave Eddie an envelope in the dark parking lot. There's only one reason I can think of for that. Some sort of deal."

"Makes sense to me. And second?"

I turned a corner. The sun was just rising. There were ghosts of fog rising from the ground. Tall trees threw shadows across the street. It was the kind of neighborhood that would look good on a postcard.

Unlike most of the team players, Lauren lived in Spokane. From what I knew, her father was a doctor. Her mother was a psychologist. They lived in a part of town with big houses and three-car garages. I could only imagine what the inside of her house looked like, what kind of furniture there was. I had an idea, though, because Lauren had her own private phone line and her own private basement suite. She had given me the number after I had agreed to help her.

"Second," I said, "let me tell you about a guy named Skids."

"The janitor's kid who's not quite all there? He's a sweet guy. What about him?"

"I think he gave me some steroid pills last night."

I slowed for a traffic light. There were no other vehicles in this quiet part of town. I watched an empty intersection as she replied.

"*Think?* You *think* he gave you some pills? Either he gave them to you or not. It doesn't take a lot of brain power to—"

"Don't get married," I told her. "You'll be doing your future husband a favor."

The light turned green. I took off without looking over at her.

"All right," she said in a quieter voice. "I shouldn't have spoken like that. But what did you mean?"

I squirmed sideways on the seat and dug one of the pills out of my pocket. "He gave me this. Maybe later we can get it to a lab or something to check it out. Skids said it would help my torn muscle heal faster. Isn't that what steroids do? Build muscles?"

"Hormones," she said. "Male hormones. The same hormones that give you pimples and make you lose your temper."

I knew that, too, but I wasn't going to tell her I had spent a couple of hours at the library to learn as much as I could.

"Skids told me the first ones were free, but his friend needed money for more. After I took the pills, I asked him who his friend was, but Skids got real quiet and edgy, like he was scared, so I stopped asking."

"Skids is a dealer's perfect choice," Lauren said. "I'll bet the dealer chooses his targets and gets Skids to make the first contact. How many people are going to turn a guy like him in? I wonder if Skids even realizes he's offered you illegal drugs? I feel so sorry for him."

I finally looked over at her. Just a quick look. She was half-frowning in thought. For some reason, it was cute, her concentration.

I didn't want to admit it. And I would never admit it to her. But she was smart.

I reminded myself I was mad at her. I told myself I didn't like the way her perfume filled the car. I tried to force my mind back to *why* she was in the car. Not on the simple fact that she was in it.

"I think," I said, "and I hate to say it, but it also makes sense that Al gets Skids to move the pills. Skids is at the rink at night when people aren't around. No one sees what's happening."

Lauren frowned deeper. "Do you think Skids is giving drugs to anyone else on the team?"

"No," I said. "I can't see that. I know the guys pretty well."

"Maybe Skids has at least offered them to other players?"

"Maybe," I said. "And maybe we'll know more after we see what happens when Eddie meets with Al."

I pointed in the backseat at a small black case under my crutches. "I've got binoculars to watch them from a distance."

"You have thought this through, haven't you."

"Yup." And I told her about another theory. I didn't think Al was making the steroids himself. Maybe Eddie and Al were going to meet the main supplier.

It turned out I was wrong. Really wrong.

We got to Eddie's billets' address twenty minutes later. We waited down the street—hardly talking—for an hour until Eddie walked out of the house toward his Mustang parked in front. Eddie was wearing a sweater and dress pants.

He got into his car without looking back at us. He did his usual squealing rubber as he took off. We followed from a distance as Eddie filled up with gas, washed his car, and stopped by a store for chocolate bars and Pepsi.

When he finally stopped and parked his car to meet Al, it wasn't in some dark alley in the bad part of town. Instead, they shook hands as they met each other in the parking lot of a church.

Eighteen

Weird," Lauren said. "A church. But in a way, it's the perfect spot to do a deal. No one would suspect anything. Should we go inside and find out who else is in on this?"

"Look at us," I said. "I'm in a sweat suit. I can't walk without crutches. You're wearing a Spokane Chiefs sweater. This is a church, not high school. Eddie and Al would spot us in ten seconds flat."

"You don't have to sound so mad," she said. "It was just a simple question. It's not like going into a church would kill you."

"Don't bet on that." I crossed my arms and shut my mouth.

She caught my mood and didn't reply.

For the next fifteen minutes, we watched as other cars and trucks filled up the parking lot. Moms in dresses and Dads in suits walked with little boys and girls, holding hands as they walked into the church.

Above them all, the morning sun had burned off the traces of fog and now hung in a clear sky. With no wind and a totally blue sky as a backdrop to the trees, it was a perfect Sunday morning. So perfect, the whole scene brought back memories.

"By the look on your face, someone pumped you full of lemon juice," Lauren said.

"If you're trying to make a joke," I said, "it didn't work."

I turned on the radio and left it on full volume. I was sitting in a car with a girl who drove me nuts, waiting outside a church to prove that a man I thought was cool was instead a drug dealer. I didn't want to talk.

Five minutes later, she turned down the volume. "I get it. Your dad. He was a preacher. This reminds you of him."

"It's not a subject I talk about." I didn't bother to turn up the radio again.

Five more minutes of silence.

"Al's a good goalie coach, isn't he?" she asked.

"The best," I answered. I lifted my hands to make a wave that took in the church. "That's why I hate him for this."

"This?"

"That he turned out to be rotten. That he's using the church to make him look good."

"And that's why you hate your dad?"

I glared at her.

She gave me a cute smile. "My mother's a psychologist. I can't help myself."

Another cute smile. "Besides, for some reason I'm

80

starting to like you. Just a little. Even though you're such a stubborn jerk."

Her smile thawed me a bit, in the hesitating way that melting snow slowly slides off a roof.

"Here's the whole story," I said. "My dad was a preacher. When my sister and I were very small, he preached at a little church. Those times are my favorite memories because he had time for us. But he was so good at preaching that his church grew. It grew so big that the church became more important to him than we were. It grew so big that he moved to television. He was good at that too. So good that buckets of money poured in from donations. So good he thought he was above any rules or laws. He helped himself to the money. He got caught. He went to jail. End of story."

"Is he sorry?" she asked.

"Doesn't matter," I said. "He ruined our family. He ruined my life."

"But if he's sorry, shouldn't you forgive him?"

"I'll never forgive him," I said, gripping the steering wheel tight with both hands. "He doesn't deserve it."

Lauren reached across. She put a hand softly over one of mine. She spoke so quiet it was almost a whisper. "But you deserve it."

For a couple of heart beats, she left her hand on mine. She finally pulled it away. She kept speaking softly.

"Give me a few minutes, okay Gump? Listen to me without putting up those big walls."

After a few seconds of silence, I nodded. I didn't look over at her. I just nodded.

"I'm going to talk about Jesus," she said, "which is funny because you grew up with a father who was a preacher."

Leaves drifted onto the windshield, making a light scratching sound above her voice.

"I told you my mother is a psychologist. Lately, she has also started to talk about Jesus. Not preaching about Him, but more like looking at what He said from a psychologist's point of view. She says in her work with troubled people, she's been using more and more of what He said. She says even if you don't want to believe He's the Son of God, His teachings make too much sense to ignore, especially for people in pain."

Lauren half laughed. "She did her best to ignore faith things because they taught her to do that at the university. But she says life is teaching her that faith is very important. After all these years, she's even thinking of going to church to learn more about Him. She says there is so much truth in Him that she can't help but wonder if everything He said about God and Himself is true."

"Wonderful story," I said in a way that let her know I meant the opposite.

"Gump, you promised you would listen."

"I'm sorry."

"So here's what I wanted to say. And it's not me speaking but my mother. She told me that if people forgive like Jesus taught they should, it sets them free."

"Right." I snorted. "Like I'm the one in jail. Not my father."

"Really? I've rarely seen you smile. You're so mad

at him that you won't let yourself enjoy anything. If that's not a kind of jail, then—"

"Look," I said. "What's my business is my—"

"You promised you'd listen. If you choose not to forgive your father, you are holding on to the hurt. The way it is now, what he did hurts you again and again, even though his actions have ended. If you could forgive him, it would be over. Not only for him but also for you. Maybe you could start smiling again."

I turned my head away from her. I was picturing the little boys and girls walking into the church with their parents. I was remembering how happy I'd been when I was that age. It made me sad now. I had a lump in my throat, and if I was going to do something stupid like cry, I didn't want her to see it.

Something in the side mirror caught my eye. It was a man about half a block behind the car, walking toward us on the other side of the street. There was something familiar about his walk. I watched until I figured it out.

It was Steve Haliburton. How did he know we were here?

Then I saw that he wasn't walking toward the Volvo station wagon. He would walk right past it. But only if he didn't see me or Lauren. If he did, we were in trouble. Even a stupid sports reporter would wonder why two Spokane Chiefs goalies were sitting together in front of a church. And Steve Haliburton was not stupid.

I turned to Lauren. I grabbed her hand. I pulled her toward me.

"What's going on?" she asked.

"Quick," I said. "Put your arms around my neck."

"What?!"

"Do it now."

She heard the seriousness in my voice. She put her arms around my neck. I pulled her close and whispered in her ear.

"You have to pretend you're my girlfriend," I said. "At least until Haliburton walks by. Keep your face turned to my face so he can't see you."

Lauren giggled. "Oh Gump," she said, like she was saying a line in a play. "You're so handsome."

Her cheek was warm against mine. It made me wish that I was handsome. And that short, wide guys might sometimes have a chance with pretty girls.

When Steve Haliburton finally walked past us, she let go.

"Your face is cute when it's red," she told me.

"Very funny," I said.

What wasn't funny was Steve Haliburton. When he got to the church parking lot, he marched straight to Al Handley's black Corvette. He opened the door, sat inside, and waited for church to end.

Nineteen

Confusing as it was, I was almost glad to see Steve get into Al's Corvette. It gave me an excuse not to think about what Lauren had said about my father. It also gave me an excuse not to think about why my face had turned red when her arms were around my neck.

"What's Steve doing?" I asked Lauren. "Any guesses?"

"If we were able to figure out something's going on," she replied, "there's no reason a reporter like Steve couldn't. Maybe he found out enough to want to ask Al about the steroids."

I snapped my fingers. "Of course! Last night he was poking around. He's on the same trail we are. This would be a huge story for him."

"If Steve does a story on this," Lauren said, "I guess that lets you off the hook."

"Huh?"

"I forced you into this because you were the only

person I could go to. But if someone else proves that Al is selling drugs . . ."

"You sound happy," I said.

"Not happy because Al will get into trouble," Lauren said. "I just want people to find out that I'm not guilty. It's horrible to be blamed for something you didn't do."

I started the car. "I understand," I said. "Trust me. I understand. Like getting blamed for putting Ex-Lax in hot chocolate."

"Not again," she said.

"Forget it. It's not a big deal if you believe me or not. Now that Steve is here, we're finished with this steroids stuff. I'll just drive you home."

The church doors opened. People began to flood out into the sunlight.

"We're not finished," she said.

For a second, I thought she wanted us to go somewhere else. Some place where we could talk. It surprised me to find out how much I liked that idea.

"We can't go yet," she continued. "What if Al goes crazy on Steve? Think about it. Instead of answering Steve's questions, Al might just drive him somewhere and, you know . . ."

"This isn't a movie plot. Al's not going to murder Steve."

"Really? If you're so sure, wait another few minutes."

I did.

Al and Eddie stepped out of the church. I pulled out my binoculars and got a close look at their faces. I couldn't tell anything from their expressions. Then, as Al got to the Corvette, I saw surprise. He turned to Eddie. Eddie shrugged.

After a few words—I wished I could read lips—Al got into his Corvette.

Eddie swaggered as he walked to his Mustang.

A few minutes later, Al began to drive away from the church with Steve beside him in the car. Eddie pulled his Mustang in behind the Corvette.

I handed the binoculars to Lauren and put the Volvo into drive.

It seemed a good idea to keep following.

Twenty

It was past eleven now. The streets were filled with enough Sunday morning traffic for us to easily stay out of sight behind a few other cars.

A few minutes later, both of their cars got on the inter-state, Highway 90. They headed toward downtown. Again, there was enough traffic that I wasn't worried about them seeing us.

They drove exactly four miles an hour above the speed limit. They stayed at that speed until the exit for Division Street. They turned north.

Division had plenty of traffic too. Not as much as on a weekday, but enough. We crossed over the Spokane River, crossed Boone Avenue and Indiana Avenue and kept going. Traffic began to thin. I had to stay farther and farther back to not be seen.

Lauren didn't say much. Probably because there wasn't much to say. Guessing about their destination was useless. We would find out when we got there.

Ten minutes later, we reached the split in Division Street at the north end of Spokane. I was hoping both cars would go right and take Highway 2. It was a busier road.

Unfortunately, they went left, to Highway 395. I had to drop back even farther. I kept three pickup trucks and a taxi between us. A few miles later, the taxi turned off. But I'd been able to let two more cars in front of me.

"I didn't expect this," Lauren said, breaking a long silence. The city was behind us. Pine trees and scattered houses lined the road.

"Me neither," I answered. "And I can't figure out why Eddie is following Al. If Al is taking Steve somewhere, shouldn't he be worried about Eddie knowing?"

A few more miles stretched to fifteen miles. I kept the Volvo nearly a half mile back.

"Keep an eye on them with the binoculars when you can," I said. "And let's hope they don't turn off when we lose them around a curve."

Another ten miles. We passed places marked by highway signs. Deer Park. Clayton.

Then we saw the highway marker for Loon Lake.

"Al's signaled a left turn," Lauren announced from behind the binoculars. "And Eddie's brake lights just flashed on."

"Loon Lake?" I said. "What's in Loon Lake?"

Nothing, as it turned out. They drove past it to a place called Springdale. At Springdale, we reached Highway 231. I expected them to turn north or south. Instead, they crossed over the highway, onto a narrow road.

"Follow?" I asked Lauren.

"We've come this far," she said. "Besides, not knowing what's happening is driving me nuts."

I followed. The road led into dense forest in the hills. There was no traffic to keep between us. I had to stay as far back as possible and hope that if they noticed the Volvo, it would only be the first time. That way, they might think we just happened to be headed in the same direction they were.

As the road continued, it got higher and higher, narrower and narrower. It seemed like we were headed nowhere. If they saw us now, they would probably think they were being followed. Much as I didn't want to, I dropped back farther. The only good news was that there were no crossroads on this lonely wilderness road. They wouldn't be turning off somewhere and losing us.

"Still curious?" I asked Lauren as we got higher and higher into the mountains.

"More," she said. "This is exactly what Al would be doing if this was a movie and he wanted to get rid of Steve."

"Sure," I said sarcastically. "And Eddie's following so he can help Al get rid of the body."

I was joking, but it hit us both at the same time. How much sense it made.

Lauren spoke slowly, as if she was as stunned as I felt. "Say Steve has been bugging Al with questions. Questions Al didn't like. So Al sets up a meeting place. Steve doesn't think he can get in trouble in a church parking lot and walks into the trap. Look at

Eddie. He's big, mean, and stupid. Who's a better person to get in on this? Especially if Al and Eddie have worked together in drug deals before this."

"I don't like it," I said. "Any of it. And I sure don't like the fact that we are so far into the mountains. This road is going nowhere fast."

As if to prove me right, the pavement ended around the next curve. We drove onto gravel and into the dust raised by the vehicles in front of us.

We slowed down.

Five miles later, so high up that when we looked back we saw an incredible view where the trees thinned, the clouds of dust hanging above the gravel road ended. I slammed on the brakes. I pointed left at a dirt road that disappeared into dense trees.

"They must have gone in there," I said. "Otherwise there would be more dust ahead."

"We've come this far," Lauren said. "How much harm could there be in going the rest of the way?"

Twenty-One

The rest of the way wasn't much farther. We drove a quarter of a mile on rough, car-rocking road that was hardly more than tire tracks. We found the Corvette and the Mustang parked in a small clearing. There was no sign of Al or Eddie or Steve.

I hit the brakes, shifted into reverse, and backed down the hill.

"Where are you going?" Lauren whispered.

"Hiding the car," I said. I turned the wheel and hid the car deep among some trees.

"Do you think they know we're here?" Lauren whispered again.

"You don't have to whisper," I said. "They would have heard our car motor long before they'll hear you."

"Oh," she said, still whispering. "Do you think they heard the motor?"

"Probably not. We were a few minutes behind them. This is a new Volvo. Very quiet."

"Good. Do you want to get out?" she asked.

"Do we have a choice? Just don't slam your door."

It took me longer than her. I had to hop on my right foot and balance myself while I got my crutches.

I stood for a moment and looked around.

This high in the mountains, the air was a lot cooler than it had been in Spokane. Sunshine slashed through openings between the trees, shining off the hood of the Volvo, leaving the back half of it in shadow. Pine scent filled the air.

Lauren walked around to my side of the car.

"Now what, Sherlock?"

I studied her nervous grin.

"You're scared, aren't you?" I asked.

"A little. How about you?"

"Nope." I grinned. "All right. A little. I'm expecting some hillbilly to step out with a shotgun and ask us what we're doing."

She shivered. "Me too. What exactly are we doing?"

"Sneaking up on Al, I guess. Trying to find out what he's doing with Steve."

She led the way back up to the clearing. It was obvious which way to go. There was a trail that led upward. At the start of the trail was a weathered sign. A warning had been carved into the sign: HIKERS, WATCH FOR DEEP MINE SHAFTS.

Lauren looked at me. I looked at her.

"Mine shafts. I hope that's the worst of our problems," I said. "You go ahead of me. I'll do my best to keep up. If you see anything, come back and get me."

"Good idea," she said.

I watched her Spokane Chiefs sweater disappear around a curve in the path.

I did my best to hobble up the mountain path with my crutches.

Good idea? Hardly. This seemed like one of the dumbest ideas I had ever had.

Twenty-Two

Although I knew Lauren was ahead of me, and the others were ahead of her, I felt totally alone. The trees and their shadows closed in on me like hundreds of stern soldiers. It was disturbing to know I couldn't run if anything happened.

The toughest part for me was the silence. Except for the wind as it sighed through the high tops of the pine trees, there was total silence. Even my footsteps on the soft dirt and pine needles were silent.

I was used to traffic. Airplanes overhead. Radio. Television. I had never heard silence that seemed heavier than a blanket.

I kept hobbling. Any second, I expected a bear to come roaring at me. I remembered articles I had read about cougars following people and jumping on them from behind. I did not like this.

I struggled upward for another five minutes. Short and wide guys who do not practice hard are not in good shape for hiking. Despite the cool air, I began to sweat.

Worse, along with my nervousness, I needed to go to the bathroom. It had been a while since I'd picked Lauren up. During the time that Eddie had been washing his car, both Lauren and I had gone into the nearby convenience store to use the washrooms. Other than that, there'd been no chance.

And now I needed to go.

I felt stupid about stopping where I was. *What if Lauren came back?*

Even though it took some effort, I moved off the path. I made sure I was mostly out of sight, but still in a place where I could watch the path for Lauren. Then I took care of business.

Just as I was zipping up, I saw the flash of someone coming down the path. I leaned out of sight and waited.

It wasn't Lauren.

It was Steve Haliburton. Sun bounced off the bald spots that his greased hair could not cover.

Steve?

Had he gotten away from Al? But what about Eddie? What about Lauren?

I was going to call out to him. Then I saw it in his hand. A pistol.

And I froze where I was.

Twenty-Three

I waited until he passed me. Then I waited much longer. Once I heard the distant sound of Al's Corvette as Steve started it, I relaxed. But only a little. Something bad was going on, and I had no idea what.

I still waited. If Steve noticed the Volvo, he might come right back. It seemed the only thing I had going for me was that Steve didn't know I was around.

But then if Steve had seen Lauren, he would expect to find the Volvo and think nothing of it. Or maybe he hadn't seen Lauren at all. Or maybe Lauren had told him about me. Or maybe . . .

I was getting dizzy from trying to think it through. I needed to be doing something, not just getting dizzy.

I had two choices. Down the path. Or up.

Down meant following Steve.

Up meant finding Lauren.

I decided to go up. If Steve had left carrying the gun, whatever he left behind couldn't be good for Lauren.

If she needed help, that was more important than anything or anywhere Steve might do or go.

Up also meant more work. Another fifteen minutes more work. I turned a corner and stepped into a small meadow. A small log cabin stood on the other side.

I stepped back into the shadows of the trees.

Was anyone inside the cabin?

I listened for voices. All I heard was the sighing of the wind and the call of a crow, echoing through the woods.

I needed to look inside the cabin. But it would be stupid to cover all that open ground to get there. Instead I had to keep going on my stupid crutches through the stupid trees all because of a stupid muscle injury.

I let that anger push me ahead as I fought to get to the cabin the hard way. Through the trees. That only took another ten minutes and five dozen branch scratches across my face.

Once I was behind the cabin, I tried to get up to a window without being seen. I got as close as I could. I finally dared to move my head to the window and peek inside.

At first, I couldn't see anything except the patch of cabin that was lit by sunlight coming through the window. Then my eyes got used to the darkness, and I saw the rest of the inside of the cabin.

What I saw looked like something from a front cover of a Hardy Boys mystery. Al Handley was tied to a chair. His wrists were tied behind his back. His legs were roped to the chair legs.

On another chair was Lauren Cross. Her hands were tied in front of her and rested in her lap. There was a rope on the floor like somebody planned to tie her legs but got interrupted.

I saw something else. Something I didn't like.

The shadow of my head made an outline on the cabin floor. If Eddie was in the cabin, he could see it easy. Is that why he hadn't finished tying Lauren up?

Just as that thought entered my mind, Eddie's face appeared in front of me on the other side of the window.

"Hey, stupid," he said to me. His voice was muffled by the glass. "Come and join us."

I pushed away from the cabin. I grabbed my crutches and made a run for it.

Eddie was right. I was stupid.

He caught me within five steps of the trees. He dragged me back to the cabin.

Twenty-Four

As he dragged me, Eddie kicked open the door. He had his arms around my neck and shoulders. Halfway through the doorway, he dropped me.

From the ground, I saw why. Lauren had left her chair and was standing near the fireplace, half turned because of the sound of the door. She had a block of firewood in her hands. Although her wrists were tied, she had gone for the only weapon she could find. If I could have run farther, Eddie would not have been back so fast. She might have had a chance to get ready.

Eddie sprinted two steps toward her. The cabin was small, and he filled most of it. He grabbed Lauren by the shoulders.

"Drop it and sit down," he shouted at her. "Or I go back and kick Gump's head in."

Lauren dropped the piece of firewood. She went back to her chair.

Eddie came back for me. He grabbed me by the collar

and yanked me to my feet. He hauled me over to the chairs and dumped me in front of them. My brace clunked on the rough wood floor as I fell on my side.

Then he grabbed another chair and set it down in front of the three of us. He sat and stared at us.

I managed to get into a sitting position. Nothing on my body hurt. It rarely does. I wondered how much damage he had done to my torn thigh muscle.

"Anybody want to tell me what's going on?" I finally asked.

"Go ahead, Al," Eddie said. "You can tell him. I won't hit you again."

I twisted my head. I hadn't had a chance to look close at Al yet. Blood trickled from his mouth.

A worried look must have crossed my face. Al winked at me and grinned. A tooth was missing from his grin, and he had blood on his gums. But Al, the storyteller who was always in a good mood, wasn't going to let it get him down. Or let it get me down. Much as it hurt to see him beat up, my heart was singing. *Al wasn't the bad guy!*

"It started a few weeks ago," Al said. He licked at a dribble of blood. "Jeff Warner came to me. He told me that Skids had offered him a way to grow muscles fast."

"Steroids," I said.

"Exactly. I knew if I went to Skids, he would deny it or be too confused to help. Plus with no way to prove anything, it would be his word against Jeff's. So I asked Jeff to keep it quiet because I wanted to find out more.

First thing I did was watch our players. I wondered if anyone on the team was taking steroids."

"Nothing wrong with it," Eddie said. He flexed his arms. "Look what it's done for me."

"It's taken away so much of your brain power," I told him, "that you're stupid enough to get involved with kidnapping people."

Eddie leaned down from his chair and smacked me across the side of my head. "Look, you fat cripple, I can hurt you worse. So keep your mouth shut."

"Jerk," Lauren said to Eddie.

Eddie hit me across the other ear. "Anything else you want to say?" he asked her.

She shook her head no. I wished I didn't have a brace on my left leg. I wished I could get to my feet and fight. I'd lose, but at least I'd be able to fight back.

Eddie grinned his ugly grin. "Besides, fatso," he said to me, "I can't be that stupid. I'm getting paid to do this. Right, Al?"

I didn't know if I was bleeding. I wasn't going to reach up with my hand to check. Not in front of Eddie.

"I guessed Eddie was on steroids," Al said, his voice tired. "Especially after he went nuts that one practice. So I met with him, trying to get him to give me the source of his drugs."

"You knew Skids wasn't smart enough to be the real source," I said.

"Right," Al agreed. "If I only stopped Skids, it would be like chopping off one arm of an octopus. I wanted to find out who was giving Skids the steroids to offer to the players."

"Steve Haliburton," I said. "It can't be anyone but him. The rest of it, though, doesn't make sense to me."

"Tell him about the money, Al." Eddie was proud of himself. "That makes sense to *me*."

"After Eddie left the team," Al began to say, "I—"

"I didn't *leave* the team," Eddie interrupted. "Don't forget it. You guys *cut* me. I should have made the team. That's why this is payback time."

"After Eddie was off the team," Al continued, "I spent time with him. I wanted to help him. I wanted him to help me."

That, of course, explained why we'd seen them together.

"Last night, Al," I said, "I saw you give Eddie something. I thought it was part of a drug deal or something."

"That's why I'm so smart," Eddie said before Al could reply. "Al wanted me to do some undercover work to get to the source. So I took his money to make him think I was on his side. But at the same time, Steve Haliburton had come to me."

"Steve paid you too?" I said.

"Steve knew Al was asking around. He wanted it stopped." Eddie laughed. "Both sides were paying me. And I could take revenge on Al for cutting me from the team. Smart, huh?"

Eddie paused. "Which reminds me," he said. He hit me across the head. "I don't like being called stupid."

Al spoke quickly, trying to get Eddie's attention away from me. "When I started to look into this, I began to find warning notes on my windshield. I didn't know who was leaving them at the time. Looking back, it's obvious who and why."

Al let out a deep breath. "Gump, I went to Steve because he was a newspaper reporter. I promised him if he helped me quietly, I would give him the full story as soon as I found out everything. I didn't know he was the supplier. He had the perfect system and wanted me to quit asking questions."

"The perfect system?" I said.

"As a reporter who traveled with the team, he was the one outsider who could be around our equipment. And it gave him the perfect excuse to travel with us into Canada."

"Canada?" This was starting to make less sense, not more.

"Canada," Al said. "Steve explained it to me on the drive up here. He buys the drugs in Canada. Steroids are illegal there, too, but Steve wanted to buy from a place so far away from Spokane that he would never get tied into anything by the Spokane police."

I thought about it. "If he was bringing drugs in from Canada, wasn't he worried about getting stopped at the border? I mean, look what happened to Lauren."

"That's just it," Al said. "The perfect system. He was using our players as mules."

I nearly said Eddie must have been one of his mules, but managed to keep my mouth shut. Even if his hits to my head didn't hurt, I guessed they were doing some damage to me.

Al continued, "In drug terms, a mule is someone who

carries the shipments. Except our players didn't know Steve was using them as mules. Starting last season, whenever we played in Canada, Steve would make arrangements to buy some steroids. After the games, he would find a time when no one was looking and drop the steroids into someone's equipment."

I nodded. "That way, even if they were caught at the border, Steve wouldn't be involved."

"Yes," Al said. "Then when the equipment was unloaded in Spokane, Skids was always there to help."

It fit. But something else was bothering me.

"Why did Lauren get caught?" I asked. "Why did Steve plant the stuff in her duffel bag and tip off the customs people?"

Al shook his head from side to side. "That was part of the warnings on the notes. I was told if I didn't stop snooping around, bad things would happen to my players. And they did."

Eddie laughed. "So Al got desperate enough to pay me to go undercover. Al didn't know Steve had already asked me for a way to get Al to a private meeting. So I took Al's money and set up a meeting."

"At a church?" I said. "Why a church?"

"Why not," Eddie said. "I knew Al went, and I thought it would get Al thinking I had turned a new leaf. It sure fooled Al. All Steve had to do was wait in or near the car and show Al the gun. Al had no choice but to drive out here."

Eddie gave me a little kick. "And that's about the end of the story, fatso."

"Not quite," a voice said from the doorway.

We all looked over. It was Steve Haliburton. He was pointing his pistol at us.

"That's right kids," he said. "Pardon me for listening in. And pardon me for disagreeing with you. The story really ends with all of you at the bottom of a mine shaft."

Twenty-Five

Hey," Eddie said, "that wasn't part of the deal. You said we'd leave them here for a few days. You said when both of us were far enough away, you'd call the police and send them here to rescue them. You didn't say nothing about killing them."

I liked Eddie's plan a lot better than Steve's.

"I changed my mind," Steve said. "Just like I changed my mind about you."

"What?" From his chair, Eddie made a move toward Steve. Steve brought the gun up and pointed it at Eddie's head.

"Sit down."

Slowly, Eddie backed into the chair.

"Yes, I said I'd get you fake I.D. and plenty of money for your escape," Steve told Eddie. "But what's easier for me? Paying you off and worrying about blackmail later or sending you to the bottom of a mine shaft with them?"

Steve moved into the cabin, keeping his gun steady. "Sorry folks. The steroids thing was the beginning of a nice little sideline. I'd gotten athletes that I cover in other sports involved. Plus players on other teams at the arena to buy. I tried without luck to bribe your trainer for medical information, hoping this season to get some Chiefs players involved. He thought I only wanted the information for articles, but I wanted to know who could use help. Still, the whole business wasn't big enough money yet to kill for. In fact, when I drove away, I believed we'd do things the way I promised Eddie. Then I changed my—"

Steve stopped as he noticed me on the floor. Eddie must have blocked me from his vision until Steve got closer.

"Gump," Steve said. "You're here too. Did Lauren talk you into this?"

I answered his question with a question. "What about Skids?"

"Skids?" Steve said. "He wants friends so bad, he'd probably help me for nothing."

"You won't hurt him," Lauren said.

Steve laughed. "He's too stupid to bother with. But you guys, I'm going to have to kill."

"All of us!" Al said. "Don't be insane!"

"Trust me," Steve said. "I gave this some thought. That's why I turned around and came back. I decided I don't want to spend the rest of my life on the run. After all, even with fake I.D. and living in a different state, I wouldn't be totally safe. If I ever got caught, that would mean years in jail. I've done stories about penitentiaries. I'd rather you guys be dead than leave you alive to send me to jail. These mine shafts are so deep, there's no chance you'll ever be found. I'll never go to jail for your murders. And by killing you, I get to keep my nice life in Spokane. And I can keep making money with my steroids scam. So, in the end, it just isn't worth it to let you live."

Sometimes, in the net, time slows down for me. Without even thinking, I know what to do. It's like some sort of instinct lets me sense the way a sequence of events can happen. It's almost like a chess game, guessing what move will lead to what reaction. Like seeing the big picture all at once, without taking time to describe it.

I had one of those moments. Knowing I would die one way or another helped me make my decision.

I rolled sideways and struggled to my feet.

"What are you doing?" Steve asked mildly.

I moved to the side so neither Lauren nor Al would be hit if Steve shot at me.

"I said, what are you doing?" Steve repeated.

"Getting ready to take the gun away from you."

Steve laughed. "Right. Even without that brace on, you couldn't get to me before I shot."

I ignored Steve.

"Eddie," I said, "stand up."

"Huh?" Eddie said.

"Stand up," I said. "Do you think it makes a difference whether you die here or at the bottom of a mine shaft? If you stand now, he's going to have to choose one of us. He can't get us both."

As I spoke, I took a limping step toward Steve. I wanted to force him to think, just for a moment or two.

From the corner of my eye, I saw movement as Eddie stood.

I took another step.

"Stop," Steve said. He pointed the gun at my thigh. "I *will* shoot."

"Eddie, if he does, you tackle him," I said.

I took another step toward Steve.

Steve pulled the trigger. It was a flat crack, not as loud as I expected. My leg wobbled. There was some dull pain in my thigh, but other than that, nothing.

I smiled at Steve. I took another step.

"Now, Eddie," I said in a calm voice.

Steve stared at me in disbelief. That disbelief saved all of us. Because Steve waited too long. He let me get too close. He couldn't turn the gun on Eddie because I'd be able to jump across the last little bit of space between us. Steve didn't even have time to lift the gun and fire into my stomach or chest.

He shot and hit my leg again.

And then Eddie was on him. Big, mean, angry Eddie.

Steve fell backward. The gun flew out of his hand toward Lauren. Lauren dove toward it.

Eddie punched at Steve, roaring with anger. Steve rolled, trying to get away.

Lauren's wrists were tied, but her fingers were free. She got both hands around the gun. She lifted her arms and fired the gun into the ceiling of the cabin. The sound froze both Eddie and Steve.

"I don't know much about guns," Lauren said, "but I'm guessing there's at least a couple of bullets left. Who wants one first?"

Eddie and Steve didn't move.

"Good," Lauren said. "Both of you stay right where you are."

Lauren handed me the gun. "Guard them while I untie Al."

"That might not be smart," I said, handing the gun back to her. "I'm not sure how much longer I can stand."

We both looked down at my leg. Blood was soaking through my sweat pants. Her face paled.

"I thought he missed you," she said.

"Keep the gun on Eddie and get him to untie Al," I said. I sat down. I was getting dizzy. "Al can tie them with the same rope. Then worry about me."

She didn't get a chance to argue with me. A wonderful dark blanket settled over me, and the world went away. With my last thoughts, I wondered if I was going to die.

Twenty-Six

For the second time, Lauren stepped into a room where I was dressed in an ugly green hospital gown. She was carrying a basket of flowers so big that it filled both her arms.

She set it on the table beside my bed.

This time, instead of just wearing a brace on my leg, I was also hooked up to tubes that dripped plasma into my blood.

"I've been at the hospital all afternoon," she said, "waiting for the doctors to let me in."

"Nice to see you," I said.

"Did anyone tell you?"

"About the rest of it? How you and Al gave me enough first aid treatment to stop the bleeding? How you and Al left those goons tied up in the cabin and drove like maniacs to get me to the hospital? How the police went back and arrested both of them?"

"Yeah," she said. "Something like that."

"No one told me," I said. "I just guessed. Why else would I be here? Alive?"

"Show off." She faked a pout.

"Not much else I can do right now."

A puzzled expression grew on her face. "I can't figure you out," she said. "You don't look tough. But you took two bullets. And what if he'd shot you in the stomach or chest? You might have been killed."

"Don't make it a big deal," I said. "I would have been just as dead if he'd thrown me to the bottom of a mine shaft. Even if he shot and killed me, at least the rest of you had a chance."

"It's still something," she said, "blocking bullets like you block hockey pucks."

"So take me to a movie someday." That slipped out before I realized what I was saying.

Her face turned red.

"I'm sorry," I said. "That was a stupid thing to say. I mean, I'd like to go on a date with you, but you shouldn't feel like you owe it to me because of what I did."

She looked at the floor.

"What's with the flowers?" I asked. I wanted a subject change. Fast. Real fast.

"Oh. They're an apology. When Eddie was tying me up before you got to the cabin, he bragged about the Ex-Lax. I feel terrible for everything I said to you."

She looked up again. "Will you forgive me?"

"Already done," I said. I grinned. "Now that you'll be cleared of the drug charges, I'm guessing you'll be back on the team. Just give me a chance to play goalie when I'm all fixed up."

"Deal."

She leaned forward to say something else, but a nurse walked into the room.

"I'm sorry, Miss," the nurse said, pushing in a trolley. "It's time to give him another shot."

The nurse turned to a tray on top of the trolley. She was wearing rubber gloves. She pulled a hypodermic needle out of the tray and held it up to the light. She squeezed a single drop out of the needle.

"Miss?" the nurse said.

"Oh," Lauren said. "You want me to leave."

"Well, I doubt this young man wants you to see exactly where he's getting this needle."

I groaned. Not because it would hurt me. But because I wasn't thrilled about a middle-aged nurse seeing my lack of suntan in a certain area of my body.

Lauren stood from her chair.

"Good-bye," I said.

"Good-bye."

Lauren left the room. I closed my eyes as the nurse gave me a shot. After that, I was all alone in my room.

I stared at the ceiling because there was little else to take my attention.

And my mind wandered to one word Lauren had said. *Forgive.*

For everything that had happened. It seemed like days had passed since we'd talked in the car parked by the church. But it had only been hours.

I thought about my injuries and thought about how my body would heal over the next weeks. I thought about how long I'd been angry at my father and how the hurt had not gone away, even though a year had passed.

Did I want to still hurt about him long after my body had healed?

For the briefest of moments, I also wondered what it would be like to visit him after not speaking to him for so long. I wondered about the happiness it would give him if I hugged him and told him I wanted to be his son again. I imagined tears on his face. And on mine.

Finally, I went back to the thought I had just before passing out in the cabin in the mountains. What if I had died? Dad would never have known something I had been too angry to admit, even to myself. He was my father, and I still loved him.

"Gump?"

Lauren was at the door. Not looking inside, but calling from the hallway.

"Yeah?"

"Is the nurse gone?" she asked. "Is everything covered up?"

"Yeah."

She stepped inside the room.

"Just wanted to tell you something," she said.

I waited.

"Yes," she said.

"Yes?"

"Yes. You know, about the movie. Yes, I want to go on a date with you. And not because I think I owe you."

Before I could say anything, she crossed the floor to my bed. She leaned down and kissed me on the cheek. Then she straightened and left the room.

I stared after her. Her perfume hung over me. I smiled.

As soon as I could get to a phone, I'd call my dad. He'd probably enjoy hearing about all this. And about Lauren.

Lightning on Ice Series

Rebel Glory

B. T. McPhee, the star defenseman of the Red Deer Rebels, likes his chances of making it as a pro. But he doesn't like the small "accidents" that may keep his team from making the playoffs—and keep him off the team. In the spotlight of high-pressure hockey, B. T. has no choice. Unless he can unravel the mystery, the team's season—and his own career—will surely end. (ISBN 0-8499-3637-3)

All-Star Pride

Hog Burnell is playing on a WHL All-Star Team touring Russia. The goal is to beat the Russian All-Stars in the best-of-seven series to be shown as a television special. Hog could use the money that will come with a series win by the WHL All-Stars. But it doesn't take Hog long to discover there's plenty more money to be made along the way . . . if he's willing to pay the price for it. (ISBN 0-8499-3638-1)

Thunderbird Spirit

Dakota Smith plays for the Seattle Thunderbirds. He's fast and smooth with a shot as deadly as most pros. Unfortunately, there are more than a few unwilling to accept a Native American in hockey. For Mike "Crazy" Keats, haunted by a troubled background that fast makes him friends with Dakota, it means hockey just got more complicated. Racial hatred takes Mike and Dakota into a web of violence and deceit that makes winning this year's championship the least of their concerns.
(ISBN 0-8499-3639-X)

Winter Hawk Star

Riley Judd is a star center for the Portland Winter Hawks. His great playing skills are exceeded only by his oversized ego, which gets in his way. Given the choice of working with street kids in roller hockey or getting kicked off the team, Judd takes what he thinks is the easy way out. Along with a teammate named Tyler Watson, he discovers that it could cost their lives to give the kids the help they really need.
(ISBN 0-8499-3640-3)

Blazer Drive

When Josh Ellroy, left-winger for the Kamloops Blazers, and his dad find more than a dozen dead cattle on the family ranch, Josh has some serious decisions to make. On one hand the Western Hockey League playoffs are ahead, plus a chance to play in the National Hockey League. On the other hand, there's a beautiful and interesting girl who believes more prize bulls will be killed. Josh is afraid of what will happen if he gets involved. As he learns more, he's afraid of what will happen if he doesn't. (ISBN 0-8499-3983-6)

Chief Honor

Lauren Cross joins the Spokane Chiefs to become the first female player on a WHL team. For Chiefs goaltender Joseph Larken, the prospect of a season in the publicity shadow of the new goalie promises to be a nightmare. Hiding behind a carefully built wall of anger, Joseph is almost relieved by the steroids scandal that knocks Lauren off the team . . . until he begins to believe she was framed. The truth makes him wish he were some place safer—like in the net facing a 110 mph slap shot. (ISBN 0-8499-3984-4)

Western Hockey League

The Western Hockey League Encourages You to Stay in School

The players of the Western Hockey League are working hard toward reaching the dream of playing in the National Hockey League.

That's not the only thing they are working hard at. They know that as hard as they work on the ice, it is important to work just as hard in the classroom. Education makes them better players and better people.

The Western Hockey League makes sure that all of its players have the opportunity to succeed all the way through high school and into college or university. Players work together with their teachers, counselors, and teams to learn both on and off the ice.

WHL players know when the going gets tough, on or off the ice, you must never give up. A good education will help you make better decisions about what to do with the puck, or what to do in life situations.

Whenever you have a question or a problem in school, ask your teacher or your counselor for help. And no matter what, STAY IN SCHOOL.